ADVANCE PRAISE

"*The Spy on the Tennessee Walker* is an eloquent and impassioned love letter to history and heroism, Southern cooking and storytelling, secret-keeping and clever sleuthing, and—above all—to smart, sassy, and fearless women. 'Write what you know' goes the old saying. Linda Lee Peterson wrote the book—again!—on smart, sassy, and fearless."

> — *New York Times*–bestselling
> author Jefferson Bass

"*The Spy on the Tennessee Walker* is deliciously entertaining! Through old letters, flashbacks, and the modern-day investigations of the San Francisco–based Fiori family, the secrets of Civil War nurse Victoria Alma Cardworthy are finally unraveled, 150 years later. Amateur sleuth Maggie Fiori is a thoroughly contemporary character, but thanks to Linda Lee Peterson's facility with historic fiction, Victoria will capture every reader's heart."

> — Naomi Hirahara, Edgar Award–winning author
> of the Mas Arai and Ellie Rush mystery series

"A captivating tale of generations-long hidden secrets of spies, forbidden love, and the Civil War. I am a Linda Lee Peterson fan."

> — Robert Dugoni, #1 Amazon and *New York
> Times*–bestselling author of *My Sister's Grave*

"Linda Lee Peterson returns with another stellar story featuring San Francisco reporter-turned-sleuth Maggie Fiori. In *The Spy on the Tennessee Walker*, Peterson moves deftly between the present day and the Civil War as she spins a compelling and moving tale of Maggie's ancestors. Expertly plotted and skillfully executed, *The Spy* is a powerful and irresistible tale that will keep you reading late into the night. Highly recommended."

— Sheldon Siegel, *New York Times*–bestselling author of the Mike Daley/Rosie Fernandez novels

THE SPY
ON THE
TENNESSEE WALKER

Linda Lee Peterson

PROSPECT
·PARK·
BOOKS

Also by Linda Lee Peterson

Edited to Death
The Devil's Interval

THE SPY ON THE
TENNESSEE WALKER

Linda Lee Peterson

Published by Prospect Park Books
2359 Lincoln Avenue
Altadena, California 91001
www.prospectparkbooks.com

Library of Congress Cataloging in Publication Data is on file with the Library of Congress

The following is for reference only:
Peterson, Linda Lee.
The Spy on the Tennessee Walker / by Linda Lee Peterson.
    pages cm
ISBN 978-1-938849-61-9 (pbk.)
1. Historical--Fiction. 2. Mystery--Investigation--Fiction. 3. Civil War--Fiction. 4. Oxford (Miss.)--Fiction. I. Title.

Cover design by Howard Grossman.
Layout by Amy Inouye, Future Studio.
Printed in the United States of America

For Captain Virginia Cardwell McDuff
and Captain Vauneta Cardwell Winthrop,
my aunt and my mother,
in honor of their distinguished service in
the Army Nurse Corps in World War II

PROLOGUE

VICTORIA, OCTOBER 1941
OXFORD, MISSISSIPPI

> *"My own experience has been that the tools I need for my trade are paper, tobacco, food, and a little whisky."*
>
> — William Faulkner in his acceptance speech for the Nobel Prize in Literature, December 10, 1950

I have been in county jails and I have been in prison. I thought I knew confinement. But there is no confinement like old age. When the bars that held me were iron, I knew with certitude that there would come a day when I could walk through the door and be a free woman again.

Today is my ninety-ninth birthday, and my days of walking through my door or any other are diminishing with alarming speed.

But today I can and will walk through the door. My great-granddaughter, who carries my middle name as her given name and shares my birthday, is coming to visit. We will go for a walk together, out to the square, and sit in the autumn sun. Sometimes we run into people we know. Our mayor always stops to greet me, and ask what scandalous novel I'm reading. And we often encounter that young

writer, Mr. William Faulkner. I have read two of his books
and liked them very much, but not enough people pay attention to him. And I believe he and his wife, Estelle, his
boyhood sweetheart, are a little too fond of their cocktails.
What's more, soon no one will call him a "young writer."
He will not see forty again. He always gives my Alma
an admiring glance, and passes some foolish compliment
about how much we resemble each other.

Two people could not look more different, and still be
alike. We both have green eyes. In that we are alike. But
she is one-and-twenty, and has a head full of red curls cor-
ralled at the nape of her neck with a black velvet ribbon.
My hair is whiter than picture-postcard snow, and I can no
longer manage to pin it up by myself. Alma will do that for
me when she arrives.

We are alike. We are both nurses. But my darling Alma
was trained in school and in clean, fitted-out hospitals. I
learned my trade (and it was a trade then, not a profes-
sion) in terrible places: the battlefields at Fredericksburg,
Vicksburg, and Manassas, and in hospitals like Chimborazo, home to the Confederate wounded. And I also cared
for Union boys, at Lincoln and Armory Square in Washington, DC. But it was those sad battlefield rides I remember most vividly, though I have spent more than seventy
years trying to forget. Even today, I can recall the precise
stinking chemistry of the battleground smell: blood, terror,
hopelessness, grief.

I would ride in on my Tennessee Walker, a proud and

handsome horse, some sixteen hands high. His name was Courage. It was good one of us had that name. I would dismount with my kit bag, and I would make that awful walk from fallen man to fallen man, while we awaited the wagons transporting the living to hospital. I had so little to offer: rudimentary skills, some precious laudanum, and bandages. Clean, cold water to slake thirst and bring fevers down. "Oh, thank you," they would say, gentlemen and tenant farmers and paupers alike. Mud and blood are great levelers of men. And when I could walk no farther, I would sink to the ground and hold the hand of the nearest dying man. "Tell me your dearest's name," I would whisper. And whatever I heard, "my wife, Margaret"; "my sweetheart, Esther"; "my little sister, Marie"; "my mother, Virginia," I would spin a fine tale around that name. About beautiful Esther who would greet her love when the war was over with plum-colored ribbons in her blond hair; about loyal Marie, who would be hanging on the garden gate, grown up but still worshipping her big brother; about Virginia, the mother who would somehow have laid hands on butter and sugar to bake her boy's homecoming cake. And the men would die with those words in their ears. Lies, all lies, but better medicine than anything I could offer.

My memory is unreliable these days. Sometimes I feel the way I do when I go to the moving-pictures with Alma. If it's a beautiful scene, I will want to hold onto it. But it slips away and I can't even recall what I loved so much on the screen. When I close my eyes at night, I still see moving-pictures. I don't always know what happened where or when, but I see so much as clear as day. A smile I loved. A song. An embrace. An adventure: going high in the sky in a balloon or the terrible sound of cannons or the crack of a rifle. I no longer have the energy to puzzle things out in a linear way, nor the courage to face all my memories. I could, I suppose, re-read my journals, but I am happier letting memories drift in for a visit and then vanish again. Most are good. Not all, certainly. But enough.

Now Alma will need some courage of her own. She is coming to tell me her news, but her mother and grand-mother have spilled the beans already. Alma is enlisting in the Army Nurse Corps, and though our United States is not yet at war, many think that time is coming very soon. Alma's mother, Jessamyn, and her grandmother Hester are distraught. They think I should interfere with Alma's decision. And while I do not like for one moment to contemplate dear Alma, the great-grandchild of my heart, being in harm's way, I will not withhold my blessing.

She is a Cardworthy woman, and we go where we are called.

Ah, I hear her key in my door. And so her adventure begins.

CHAPTER 1

MAGGIE, 2014
OAKLAND, CALIFORNIA

Sometimes you walk in the front door and there's something awaiting you other than the chaos of a one-dog, one-cat, two-boy, one-husband household. Sometimes, there are sounds and smells of dinner cooking (ten percent of the time); sometimes the younger, non-teenage member of the household, that would be Zach, age ten, will be lying in wait to deliver a bone-crushing hug and an "I love you, Mommy" (fifteen percent of the time, though dwindling as the teenage years draw ever closer); and sometimes there's a nice surprise: banana bread from a neighbor, flowers that Michael has sent for some mysterious husbandly reason, or — very, very, very occasionally — a piece of interesting mail (five percent of the time).

It was a five-percent evening. A large box sat on the dining room table, addressed to me, Mrs. Michael Fiori, in a hand I'd known since childhood, the elegant swoops and swirls of my mother's youngest sister, Aunt Phoebe. Oxford, Mississippi, was the return address.

I am a sucker for a package, especially one sent by an actual person and not an anonymous fulfillment picker at an unnamed Amazon warehouse. I kicked off my shoes, padded into the kitchen, was shocked, shocked, shocked to find the scissors precisely where they were supposed to be, and within a few minutes, had snipped and ripped my way into the box. On top was a note from Uncle Beau, Aunt Phoebe's husband and the family genealogist.

Maggie, dear, I thought you might like a reminder of how the generations unfolded on your mother's side.

Below his note was a string of names, starting with my great-great-great-grandmother Victoria Cardworthy, 1841–1942, and ending with me.

Victoria Alma Cardworthy Stern, 1841–1942
    (Maggie's great-great-great-grandmother)
Victoria's daughter Hester, 1867–1948
    (Maggie's great-great-grandmother)
Victoria's granddaughter Jessamyn Alma,
    1897–1965 (Maggie's great-grandmother)
Victoria's great-granddaughter Alma,
    1919–2012, married to Morris (Maggie's
    grandmother)
Victoria's great-great-granddaughter Isabella,
    1945– (Maggie's mother)
Victoria's great-great-great-granddaughter,
    Maggie Stern Fiori, 1974–

Underneath the note was a carefully bubble-wrapped double frame. I tore off the bubble wrap and touched my finger gently to the glass. Two women faced each other in a hinged frame. On the right, my glamorous Grandmama Alma. She was waving to someone and laughing in sheer delight. I wasn't sure of the year, but she already had captain's bars on her olive uniform, so it had to be late in the war. Funny how Korea, Vietnam, Iraq, and Afghanistan have all done their terrible damage, but I still think of World War II as "The War." It was my grandparents' war, and both Alma and Morris served in the military. When Grandmama Alma was buried two years ago, her casket had been draped in a flag. Until then, I had seen that sight only in the movies or on television, but there it was, in real life. And I'd watched my boys, sitting on either side of me clutching my hands, wondering at what they were seeing. We sat in silent witness as two sober-faced, handsome young men in uniform folded the flag in a precise triangle and presented it with great reverence to my grandfather.

I had an album and a thumb drive full of photos of both Grandmama Alma and Papa Morris, but I'd never seen this photo. And now Papa Morris's grip on his memory was slipping away. I think the best part of him was already wandering the world, looking for Alma and longing to be together again.

In the facing frame was a daguerreotype of a serious woman astride a horse. She had on a long skirt, and I could see rugged, rough-and-ready boots in the stirrups. And it looked as if she'd just come to a stop. Her bonnet had fallen back on her neck, held on with a tattered sash tied under her chin.

"Mom, is that you? Were you dressed up for some weird costume party? Or Halloween?" I jumped. I hadn't even heard Josh, not the quietest of galumphing fifteen-year-olds, come into the kitchen.

"Hi, honey," I said, putting the frame down. "How was your day?"

He shrugged. "You know. The usual. Blah blah blah.

Boring, boring, boring. Here's the big news: Somebody finally snitched about Mr. Avery's little dope enterprise."

"What? The French teacher? Are you serious?"

"Yeah. Everybody knew. Like he went to Morocco for every vacation on some pathetic teacher's salary? He was running a fine little *j'ne sai* excellent-shit import-export operation out of there."

"Mr. Avery?!?"

He made a current universal teenage gesture, pantomiming taking a pill and swallowing it down. "Chill pill, Mom. I wasn't one of his customers."

"Oh, good," I said faintly. "So reassuring to know."

He picked up the frame. "Seriously, what's the deal? Did you get a new app to make yourself look like Annie Oakley?"

I pointed at the woman on the horse. "You think that's me?"

"It is you," he said. "Same eyes, same hair. And by the way, even if you're on horseback for some lame reason, you need some product in that hair." He looked thoughtful. "I could get Lexie to help you." Lexie. The Cupcake. The one Michael called the strumpet-of-the-month. She dressed like catastrophe with a capital C and it stands for cleavage, but she was Josh's crush, so I had to hold, bite, imprison, and otherwise restrain my tongue.

"That would be nice," I said carefully. "I'd love to hear what product Lexie uses on her hair. It's certainly very...."

"Hot. Even her hair looks hot." Josh sighed. He was smitten.

"Well, honey," I said. "I hate to break to it you, but your mom just may never have hot hair, whatever that is." I heard myself sounding like a killjoy. "I could try Lexie's product," I said, brightly. "You know, give your dad a thrill to be hanging out with someone who has 'hot hair.'" He winced.

I turned back to the mystery photo, the one that Josh identified as me. "And sorry, that's not me. I'm not sure who it is, but the other photo is definitely your Great-Grandmama Alma."

"She was hot," he said, "in her day. Papa Morris told me. Plus, remember what great kreplach she used to make? Plus, man oh man, she had good stories about World War II. All that shit...."

"Perhaps a different word."

"Yeah, well, all that *stuff* about smuggling whiskey across the border in perfume bottles...."

"You remember those stories?"

"Yeah, of course. She had *adventures*. She went to war and she saved people's lives. And she was, you know, like a big shot for that time. She was a captain."

I stared at Josh. Surprises every day. "I had no idea you were so interested in Grandmama Alma's stories."

Josh sighed, "I'm *interested* in stuff that's interesting," he said with the long-suffering patience of a teenager who has to deconstruct information for dimwitted adults. "Ninety percent of which does not happen at school." He picked up the double frame again. "You're sure you're not that lady on the horse, huh? Like it was a costume and you just forgot you dressed up like that? She's your doppelglanger."

"Nice vocabulary," I said distractedly, "but the word

is actually *doppelganger*. Definitely the right idea, though. Doppelgangers are ghostly versions of ourselves, and whoever this woman is, she must be a ghost by now."

I put my arm around Josh again and we looked at the photo together. Mr. Standoffish tolerated me for a minute, then I could tell he was looking to shrug me off. "I do see what you mean," I said. "Whoever that woman was, we do look as if we could be twins." In fact, looking at the mystery woman on the very tall horse was a little like looking into the mirror.

"Call Aunt Phoebe," said Josh. "Maybe Uncle Beau knows. He's into all that genealogy stuff."

"Splendid idea."

"All my ideas are splendid, Mom. Like how this summer Lexie and I should climb Half Dome."

"Splendid idea, but the answer is no, *non, nyet, nein*."

"Really? 'Cause Dad says he's open to a conversation."

"As am I. Open to conversations about almost anything — world peace, hair-care products, Mr. Avery's illegal entrepreneurship, emerging economies, all the many ways I approve of Justin Timberlake. Just not a conversation about you, Lexie, and Half Dome." I could see Josh deciding if this was the moment for sweet-talking, negotiation, or sullen retreat. He gave me an appraising look, turned on his heel, and headed upstairs. Another triumph of inept teenage parenting. Was there a manual somewhere?

I put the framed photos on top of the carved mahogany sideboard. The sideboard had been Grandmama Alma's, and the photos looked right at home. I gathered up the papers to take out to recycling, then stopped. There was something else in the package, I shook it gently, and a small, soft, leather-bound book slipped onto the table. I picked it up and it rested perfectly in my hand. Dark, mottled red cover, with a tarnished gold-stamped oval and the words "Drum-Taps" inside the oval. On the flyleaf I read, "To my friend and fellow wound-dresser, Victoria Alma Cardworthy. We are bound forever by love, blood, and grief."

"Walt Whitman," I said aloud. "Walt Whitman inscribed this for my great-great-great-grandmother."

CHAPTER 2

VICTORIA'S JOURNAL, 1862

No one likes to see me ride in on Courage. It's not the horse, it's the fact that I'm a woman on a horse when horses have been conscripted for all but military needs. Well, perhaps I exaggerate. Most of my fellow nurses back at the hospital give me a sly look. They think I have some friends in high places. "I do," I say tartly, when they make that accusation, "and a fair measure of friends in low places as well." And that ends the conversation. I am not a great one for sharing personal information. And besides, few of the nurses and matrons at the hospital are willing to do what I do — walk among the wounded and the dead still on the battlefield, doing what I can until they can be moved to hospital or laid to their rest. The women of the hospital are content to leave that task to Courage and me.

I am what my friend Walter Whitman calls "a proper wound-dresser." He, on the other hand, calls himself a mere "visitor and consolatory." We met after the horrific December battle of Fredericksburg, when despite General Burnside's ambitious plans, and the efforts of the valiant boys of the Army of the Potomac, and the frontal assault on Marye's Heights by Major Generals Sumner and Hooker and their men, the Union forces were badly out-maneuvered. When the terrible dark smoke finally cleared, the Union had suffered more than twice as many casualties as the Confederates. Governor Andrew Curtin of Pennsylvania visited the battlefield and went directly to the White House. He reported to President Lincoln, "It was not a battle, it was a butchery."

CHAPTER 3

MAGGIE
OAKLAND

"Josh," I called upstairs, trying to curry a little favor. "Want to see if Lexie can come for dinner? Dad's making paella tonight."

Moment of silence. I could almost hear those gears turning, wondering what I was up to. "Sure," he said. "I'll text and see if she's free. And Mom, call Aunt Phoebe. I want to know what's up with those pictures."

Phoebe, still the gentle reigning queen and observer of Oxford social life, was home. I put her on speaker so I could chop onions and peppers for Michael's paella while we talked.

"Aunt Phoebe, thank you for the package."

"Glad it arrived, darlin'. I remember when your grandmother died and your mother and I swore we would not leave all those boxes and bins of stuff for our children to deal with."

"Oh, I don't have to worry about it," I said, wielding the chef's knife and squinting through the onion glasses to try to miss adding a little finger into the *mise-en-place* for Michael. "Josh has already told us he and Zach are going to back a van up to the house when we go to the great beyond and send it all to the Alameda Flea Market."

"Not Alma's carved mahogany dining table! It looks so wonderful in your house."

"I couldn't agree with you more," I said sadly. "But get this — the boys say they're afraid of the legs."

"Oh, those beautiful lion feet," said Phoebe. "Well, that's a shame, honey, but you know every generation has to find its own way. My daughter-in-law has a bright orange table with lime-green chairs in her dining room, and I have to say, it's either really cheerful or really bilious, I just can't figure out which. I think it's made of resin. Is that right? I thought that was the powdery material ballerinas put on their shoes. Do you know, honey?"

I wasn't sure which question to answer. "I think dancers use rosin, Auntie Phoebe. But it does sound like resin, and I think people do use resin for furniture. It's in all the cool lofts in San Francisco."

"Well, I'm just trying to maintain an open mind and keep up with you young people," she said. "But tell me, Miss Maggie, did you love those photos I sent? Actually, I think one is a — how do you pronounce it? — daguerreotype."

"So, there's the one of Alma, right? I recognized her right away, and then there's the one of the woman on the horse."

"Oh, honey, I had to send that to you when I found it out in the henhouse. I'm pretty sure that's your great-great-great-grandmother Victoria."

"She's been in the henhouse all these years?"

"You know, there aren't any hens in there anymore. And I'd been trying to get your Uncle Beau to move all that genealogical folderol he messes with all the time out, out, out of the house." In her ongoing battle to control disorder, Phoebe explained, they had the henhouse insulated and painted, and they added a bathroom so it could be used as a guesthouse to accommodate the unending stream of visitors they hosted, especially during Ole Miss football season. Fending off disorder meant endless vigilance, according to Phoebe. "Every time Beau adds some other treasure to the henhouse, I make him take something out. He brought that double-frame photo in for me to see, along with the little book. I took one look and said, 'If that's Victoria, Maggie is her spitting image, so these things should go directly to her.'" Aunt Phoebe took a breath.

I put the knife down. Maybe the onion glasses were defective. I pulled them off and swiped the tears away.

"Maggie, did I lose you, sugah?"

"No, Aunt Phoebe, I think you found something wonderful, and I am so touched you sent it to me."

"Really? Well, I loved those photos and thought you should have them. And the book was just in the box with the photos. And you know, since your grandmother was a nurse and I think that Victoria was a nurse, too, I figured that funny old book — what's it called?"

"*Drum-Taps*," I said. "Phoebe, if this is what I think it is, it's really valuable."

"Well, then, honey, it's found the right home."

"No, I mean, like it should go to a museum or something."

Phoebe laughed. "That's exactly what I call Beau's henhouse, 'the museum.' But nobody ever comes to visit it."

I picked up the knife again.

"Maggie, are you still there?"

"I am," I said. "Just thinking. You know what, it *is* a shame nobody comes to visit the Henhouse Museum. I think I want to remedy that situation. You tell Uncle Beau that if you'll have me, I'll come for a long weekend, and I want him to be my personal docent and guide me through the museum."

"Just a second, honey, Beau wants to say hey to you."

In a moment Beau's gravelly voice rumbled through the phone. As soon as I heard him, I remembered that when I was little, I thought that when people talked about the Mississippi as "Old Man River," they were talking about Uncle Beau.

"Miss Maggie," said Uncle Beau, "you took receipt of Phoebe's package? You know that woman is happy every single time she ships something out of the henhouse."

"Well, she made me very, very happy, Uncle Beau. And I realize that I want to know more about what all you've got in the henhouse."

I heard myself saying "what all" and realized that once again the sheer seductiveness of Southern language had crept into my accent-less California speech.

"Honey, I would be honored to give you my personal twenty-five-cent tour."

"I want the whole dollar tour, Uncle Beau. And I really want to know more about Victoria."

Silence. "Well, now, I know Phoebe sent you that photo because you really do look just like her," he said. "But...."

"But what?"

"Well, you know, we just don't have a lot of information."

"*You* don't have a lot of information? You're the most tireless genealogist in the family."

"That is true," he said. "But Victoria had a bit of a cloudy past, I'm afraid."

"Okay, you just made me more interested."

"Well, we'll see when you get here. Just so you know, your double spent some time in prison."

"Now my interest level is on red alert," I said. "I'll email you and Aunt Phoebe as soon as I can figure out a time to come, and you can let me know if it works for you."

"We'll make it work, Miss Maggie. And comin' on a weekend is perfect because you know the Egg Bowl is comin' up soon, and you could see all the cousins."

The Egg Bowl. Ah, yes, the showdown between Ole Miss, aka the University of Mississippi, and chief rival Mississippi State.

Unlike California college football games, where fans show up in team colors on top, jeans or board shorts on the bottom, depending on the weather, the Egg Bowl means blazers and ties for the gentlemen and pretty polished cotton dresses or skirts and sweaters for the ladies, along with a requisite string of pearls. "I'll pack Mama's pearls," I said.

I could hear Phoebe shouting instructions: "Beau, tell Maggie to bring a dress." I sighed. Much as I loved my family, the South is, as L.P. Hartley said about the past, a foreign country.

"Hey," I said, "I heard that the powers-that-be at Ole Miss sent old Colonel Reb into mascot retirement."

Uncle Beau gave a dry cough. "Yes, well, those powers-that-be can do all they want. And you're right, the official mascot is now the Rebel Black Bear. But you know, things don't move at warp speed here in the South, honey, so if you're looking for a Colonel Reb piece of regalia, I'm either happy — or sorry — to tell you, there's plenty of that stuff still around. This just isn't California, honey. You all have such a, ahh...*variety* of the human condition out west."

"You have plenty of variety, too," I said. "Oxford is a university town, after all."

"Oh, you are so right, honey. The young gentleman who cuts my hair, or what's left of it, is an Ole Miss senior, and he came all the way from Pakistan to go to school in little old Oxford."

"Global, global, global. Even Oxford, Mississippi, is an international mecca." I glanced at the clock. "I've got to get back to my cutting board, Uncle Beau. Tell Auntie Phoebe I said thanks again, and I can't wait to see you both and to tour the historically significant Henhouse Museum."

CHAPTER 4

VICTORIA'S JOURNAL, 1862

Bearing the bandages, water, and sponge,
Straight and swift to my wounded I go,
Where they lie on the ground after the battle
  brought in,
Where their priceless blood reddens the grass,
  the ground,
Or to the rows of the hospital tent, or under
  the roof'd hospital,
To the long rows of cots up and down each side
  I return,
To each and all one after another I draw near,
  not one do I miss

— "The Wound-Dresser," Walt Whitman

We met because of our brothers, Walter and I. When he believed that his beloved brother George, a volunteer of the Fifty-first New-York Volunteers, led by Colonel Edward Ferrero, had been injured in the Battle of Fredericksburg, Walter left his home in Brooklyn and began the long journey south to find George. He walked the rows of beds in Washington, DC, hospitals looking for his brother's face, shaken and worried that the worst had happened and that George was already in the ground.

There are so few stories with happy endings in wartime, but Walter's search was to be one of those occasions. He found his brother at an inn near the hospital. George's injuries had been quite minor, and he was recovering among friends in similar situations at a rough but comfortable hostelry.

"I traveled with such trepidation, Miss Victoria. I was afraid of what I might find, and dreading how to tell the news to my family. And there, to my astonishment, was George, slouching at the table and playing cards with his compatriots."

I, too, had traveled to see my brother, but in the beginning I could not tell Walter where I had found him. I did not know whom I could trust. For the truth of the matter was that my brother wore Confederate gray, and when I found him at the Chimborazo Hospital in Richmond, Virginia, my Jeremiah was not nearly as fortunate as Walter's brother George. Jeremiah had already lost a leg, amputated when the wicked, fast-moving gangrene had begun its terrible journey up, up, up his right leg. When I stopped at his bed, he was raving with night terrors. "Leave me alone, leave me alone. I need both legs to plow!" he was crying out. "Go away with your terrible saws!" I sat all night with him, waiting for first light, putting clean, cool, damp rags on his forehead.

By morning, the fever had broken. He opened his eyes and I said, "Hello, my darling brother."

And then he wept. The indefatigable, adored big brother God had provided me, full of courage and good humor. The one who made sure I had partners at every dance, the one who stood up to my parents when I began to study the art and science of nursing, the one who was afraid of no man and no battle.

"Vic," he whispered. I knelt on the floor next to his bed, so I could hear him. "You should leave me, I am good for nothing."

I looked at him and I felt some powerful mix of anger and resolve fill my heart. "You are good for everything, Jeremiah," I said. "And if you do not put your mind and heart and body to recovery, then I will never give you a moment's peace. I will come back to your bedside with Mother and Father. Then I will bring your sweetheart. And then," I said, warming to my campaign, "I will bring Cannonball, and when he sees you in this reduced state, he will not know the brave master he once had."

Jeremiah blinked and raised himself up on one elbow. "My dog? You will not bring my dog here!"

"I will," I said, "because it is cruel for him to think you are never coming home. So, I say, if you have surrendered to these…these…inconsequential Yankees, then Cannonball should see you in your hour of despair, and…failure!" I got to my feet. "Shall I go fetch them all now? Mother, Father, Elizabeth, and Cannonball, to see how the mighty have fallen?"

Jeremiah collapsed back onto the bed and began to laugh. "You are the worst nurse a man must endure. Where is the comfort? Where is the sympathy? Where is the gentle hand upon my brow?"

I scowled at him. And then I melted, as I always did. No matter what, Jeremiah makes me laugh. "All right, sirrah. I will not threaten you with Mother, Father, and the... spectacularly admirable Miss Elizabeth Townsend."

Jeremiah caught my hand. "But you will threaten me with my own dog?"

"Oh, yes, I most certainly will."

Jeremiah grinned at me. "You have bullied and badgered me into feeling better, Vic. You are a trickster and a witch, but you are the best medicine possible."

And so I sat down again, and we began to make a plan for Jeremiah's recovery.

Just a few months later, I found myself in the Armory Hospital in Washington, and Walter and I began our friendship. "We have a brother-and-sister bond," Walter said. "We made journeys to care for our brothers, and in so doing, we made a bond that could not be broken." I had always considered a promise like that to be sheer hyperbole, but when it mattered, Walter proved me wrong.

CHAPTER 5

MAGGIE
OAKLAND

The great chef Michael Fiori swept into the kitchen and did all the showboat work for the paella. He did kiss his sous chef in gratitude for all the menial chopping I had done, changed Pandora from the Billie Holiday station to the CeeLo Green *Fuck You* station, and proceeded to report on how brilliantly he had outwitted some poor government tax lawyer in locking up even richer benefits for his philanthropically minded, but still a little greedy, client.

"Okay," I said. "You've now used the word 'brilliant' to refer to your IRS-evading machinations not once, not twice, but three times. Does that mean this was brilliance of a whole new world order?"

"It does," beamed Michael, "and cut me some slack, *cara*. How often do the good guys win?"

"Well, my love, when you are running the gunboats, it appears the good guys always win."

"Ain't it the truth?" he crowed as he dumped fresh clams onto the saffron-infused rice. "Call those boys to dinner, Maggie. It's time for them to see their dad be brilliant in the kitchen, and those clams are opening in front of our very eyes."

"Hey, what about honor and glory to the lowly chopper and dicer?" I asked, heading for the stairs.

"You get to sup with the chef. That should be plenty of reward for any kitchen help."

I stuck my head back in the kitchen. "You, Michael Fiori, are insufferable."

"You're right. And that's why you find me so irresistible."

In the dining room, Josh was at his most tragic, removing the extra place he'd set for Lexie. "She can't come," he said. "Her stupid parents are taking her to some dumb dinner in Berkeley." He sighed and collapsed in his chair, wiped out by disappointment. Apparently I'd forgotten just how exhausting young love can be. To make matters worse, I was in horrible, unfeeling mother mode — squelching Josh's attempt to reopen the discussion of climbing Half Dome with Lexie and reminding Zach not to feed Raider, our aging German shepherd, under the table for approximately the ten thousandth time. Mom, the perennial spoilsport.

"Hey," I said. "Delicious paella, Michael. And we got an interesting package in the mail today. Josh, would you go get it?" Josh had regained some small measure of energy simply by shoveling in three generous servings of paella. Marginally restored, he went over to the sideboard and brought the double-framed pictures Phoebe had sent and put them in front of Michael.

"Who do you see, Dad?" he asked.

"Grandma Alma," he said without hesitation. "But... who's this?"

"Who does it look like?"

Michael looked at the photo of Victoria and looked

across the table at me. "It's Mom," he said. He put the frame down and picked up his glass of wine. "Pretty slick Photoshopping. You look like somebody out of the nineteenth century."

"Wrong, as usual," snapped Josh, rejuvenated by the opportunity to correct a grown-up.

Michael looked at the photo and back at me. "Well, Annie Oakley — if it's not some touched-up version of you on the horse, who is it?"

"That," I said, "is exactly what I'd like to know. And," I said, swirling the last of the light Spanish red around in my glass, "that's why I want us to go to Oxford to visit the Cardworthy Henhouse Museum."

Michael did his eyebrow-raising trick. "Oh, tell me more. Just don't tell me I have to show up at one of those football games in a blue blazer and rep tie."

"You do, and you will," I said. "And just FYI, since both you and Josh keep throwing Annie Oakley into the discussion, I'd like to point out that she came from a different generation than my great-great-great-grand-mother. Victoria was born in 1841, Annie Oakley was born nearly twenty years later — 1860, I believe."

Silence fell around the table. "Mom," said Zach in a stage whisper. "I think you're being a know-it-all again."

CHAPTER 6

MAGGIE
SMALL TOWN *OFFICE, SAN FRANCISCO*

> *"It [California] is the land where the fabled Aladdin's Lamp lies buried and she [San Francisco] is the new Aladdin who shall seize it from its obscurity and summon the genie and command him to crown her with power and greatness and bring to her feet the hoarded treasures of the earth."*
>
> — Mark Twain

Hoyt runs a damn fine story meeting at *Small Town*. For a man who's soft-spoken, who still rises when a woman enters the room, and who reminds me of my mother's family, with that leisurely Mississippi (pronounced "Mi'-sip-ee" by the natives) drawl that sounds like a gentle waltz around colloquial Southern English, there is no nonsense at Hoyt's core. The trains run on time, and so do the writers, designers, copyeditors, and a small, rotating army of freelance photographers and illustrators. All thanks to Hoyt, who is unshakably polite and indisputably no-nonsense. I'm the editor-in-chief, but without Hoyt's shepherding, nagging, and constant surveillance, nothing substantive would get done.

It was the usual suspects around the table: Andrea "Starchy" Storch, New England's preppy gift to journalism, who did features and covered film and theater; designer Linda Quoc, dressed, as always, head to toe in black; Puck Morris, scourge of the music beat; and a couple of eager-beaver young writers who represented the sensibility of youth. They managed the online content of *Small Town* and wondered why *any* piece of writing would be longer than a tweet. Calvin Bright rounded out the team by wearing multiple hats: most favored *Small Town* photographer and sweetheart of Starchy Storch. Just two preppy sweethearts who bonded over Burberry and signet rings.

Hoyt rapped on the stained tabletop in the conference room. "My friends, we are gathered," he said. "And now, once more into the fray!"

Calvin made an elaborate show of examining his ten-million-thread-count cuffs, all meant to distract us from the fact that he was inching his hand down to Andrea's knee. Puck was building a mini tower of his signature hockey pucks, all of which bore the inscription, "Pucked by Morris," sent as an advance warning to some unsuspecting musician or group when he was readying a particularly vitriolic review.

"The sight of that growing edifice does not fill me with joy, Mr. Morris," said Hoyt. "I know you have submitted only two reviews in the upcoming issue, so even if you loathe both the groups, you can't possibly need all those pucks."

"Oh, man," said Puck. "One of these groups is so godawful, I may send a whole box of pucks. One for being lousy guitarists, one for being derivative, one for forgetting to tune ahead of time, and one for really creepy red Spandex getups."

"I predict a small avalanche of outraged letters from the Spandex wearers," said Hoyt.

"Don't you worry, big guy," said Puck. "I know these guys can't read music, and I'm pretty sure they can't read words either. They'll never know what hit 'em."

Hoyt glanced at me, looking for help. "Puck," I said, "you know it's not your job to hate everything, right?"

Puck sat up very straight, thereby adding a good three-quarters of an inch to his not-quite-five-and-a-half-foot frame. "The Puck is mightier than the sword," he pronounced. "I calls 'em as I sees 'em."

"We are reminded," said Hoyt, "of Alice Roosevelt Longworth's embroidered throw cushion, 'If you haven't got anything nice to say about anybody, come sit next to me.'"

The rest of the story meeting evolved as usual: writers pitching, Hoyt catching, me reporting out on a couple of major features in the hands of outside writers, reviewers previewing what they might like or loathe, Linda taking us through the digital portfolio of hot new conceptual photographers for a story on the Twitterization of Hayes Valley.

Since Twitter and Google had moved into the city proper, complete with buses that looked as if they were going to and from summer camp, the real estate prices in San Francisco — always ridiculous — had become laughable. Young people regularly showed up at completely unremarkable one-bedroom apartments, fiercely outbidding each other until a round of all-cash offers for million-dollar apartments went into smack-down. The restaurant scene was in a constant state of churn — tapas were down, prix-fixe was up, insects were ingredients (and not by accident), and edible foam was back. Bacon doughnuts were about to become passé.

"We will have one moment of silence," said Andrea, "for the way Hayes Valley used to be — seedy, weird, not very clean, and dispensing botulism out of every eatery. Come on, guys, let's not romanticize squalor."

And with that we were back to the story list. After the meeting I followed Hoyt down to his office.

"Guess where I'm going next week?" I asked.

"To find some backup lawyers for the next time Puck sends some ungifted musician around the bend?"

I laughed. "Not yet."

"Then I'm a lost ball in tall grass. Where are you going, Maggie, and why isn't it on the vacation schedule?"

"Oops, sorry. And it's really just a long weekend, but I'm going to your hometown: Oxford, Mississippi."

"Better you than me. One of the blond cousins getting married?"

"Research. I'm checking out a new museum — the Cardworthy Henhouse Museum, owned and operated by my aunt and uncle and open only when they are in residence."

"And what is prompting this visit?"

I opened my briefcase and put the double-frame photo on Hoyt's desk. He pulled the frame close for a look, put it down, and looked at me.

"Who are these fine-looking ladies?"

"One is my grandmother Alma, the one in the uniform. I don't know for sure who the other woman is, and that's why I'm going to Oxford."

"Do the proprietors of the Henhouse Museum know who she is?"

"They're vague, but apparently she's my great-great-great-grandmother, and she was a nurse in the Civil War."

"Or as my people used to call it, 'the War Between the States,'" said Hoyt. "Well, whoever she was, she is a beautiful woman, and she looks as though nothing would stand in her way. My guess is you and she have more in common than a handsome head full of curls."

"What was it like, Hoyt? Growing up in Oxford? I've been going there all my life, off and on, to visit family, but I have no sense of what it's really like to live there."

Hoyt closed his eyes. "You know, Maggie, I can still conjure what the place smells like."

"Good or bad?"

"Oh, in spring, when the lilacs are coming into bloom, and the heat warms up the jasmine and honeysuckle, there's nothing like it. You can get drunk."

"I love lilacs," I said, "and we can't grow them very well in California."

"No," he said, "they need hardship, a good cold frost, to thrive come spring. Most things do better with a little hardship. You know what I was remembering about the lilacs when I was a boy? I was coming home from school one day, and we had just read about the death of Lincoln, so our teacher had us memorize Walt Whitman's poem, "When Lilacs Last in the Dooryard Bloom'd," and I passed Miz Sorrelli's house, and the fragrance of those lilacs — purple ones and white ones, lining her fence — almost knocked me down. It was as if Walt Whitman himself had planted them for me as an extracurricular enhancement to his grieving poem."

"We memorized that poem, too. I'm not sure kids do that anymore."

"Stays with you."

And remarkably, that beautiful poem of love and grief came into my head.

"When lilacs last in the door-yard bloom'd,
And the great star early droop'd in the western
  sky in the night,
I mourn'd—and yet shall mourn with ever-
  returning spring.

O ever-returning spring! trinity sure to me you
  bring;
Lilac blooming perennial, and drooping star in
  the west,
And thought of him I love."

"Brava," said Hoyt. "And then Miz Sorrelli came out and saw me burying my nose in her lilacs. She said, 'Aren't they just glorious?' sounding exactly like Amanda Wingfield in *The Glass Menagerie*, although not nearly so crazy and self-aggrandizing."

I laughed. "Oh, when Amanda rhapsodizes about the jonquils that all her gentlemen callers brought her, that's what you mean?"

"Exactly right. And then Miz Sorrelli reached right into her apron pocket and pulled out some shears, clipped me a big bunch of lilacs, and wrapped the ends in a faded tea towel she fished out of another pocket, and handed the entire thing over to me.

"She told me to take the bouquet to my mama with her regards and congratulations for raising a son who knew enough to stop and worship at Mother Nature's altar."

"I love that story," I said.

"Me, too," said Hoyt. "That's the best part of small Southern towns, the kindness of relative strangers. And I didn't deconstruct all this when I was a kid, but I knew that Miz Sorrelli was a lady who lived a far grander life than we did. She had a beautiful house near the square, and people called her a 'rich widow.' But I just remember that she was always out in that front garden or the back garden, doing her own hard work with a hoe. And she was kind to me. I think she knew that we lived pretty hand-to-mouth, tenant farming not being venture capital and all." He raised an eyebrow at me. "Well, isn't that more of a story than you wanted to hear?"

"I always like hearing your stories. And you've put me in the right mood for this trip. I feel so fish-out-of-water when I go see my mother's relations. It's like I'm going on a field trip to the Old Curiosity Shop; everything seems so strange."

"Such as?"

"Oh, *everything*. I love my family, but it's 'Miss Maggie,' this, and the endless discussion of who was or was not First Runner-up in the Maid of Cotton competition. I mean, when you're forty years old, are you're still thinking of yourself as in the market for a tiara? And the clothes and full makeup to go to the Piggly Wiggly!"

Hoyt shook his head. "Honey, this is your family, and you're going on a visit. You're not an anthropologist analyzing the tribal patterns of a lost colony. And

I would like to remind you that those Maids of Cotton were very hardworking young women. They represented the cotton industry not just in the South but in other cotton-growing states, like California."

I snorted. "Anthropology is exactly what I'm doing! Or at least that's always what I catch myself thinking about. You cannot imagine the depth and complexity of the conversations about handbags among my young cousins."

"On the other hand, if memory serves, that Maid of Cotton deal ended altogether in 1993, when the Cotton Council folks decided there wasn't enough juice left in the whole competition. Plus, there is the food." We both fell silent for a few moments. "I'll tell you what I'm thinking about if you'll tell me what you're thinking about."

"Fried chicken," I said. "Cheese straws."

"Hmmm...now that sounds fine, although I do think of cheese straws as food for the ladies. But I'm thinking about the cornbread sticks my grandmother made."

"In a black iron pan, with molded sides so that the sticks came out looking like little ears of corn?"

"I have that very pan."

"For a man who got out of Oxford the minute you could, you're sounding downright nostalgic."

"Oh, no — I miss my family, I miss the food, and I do miss the good manners, but I don't miss much else about the South. It always felt very feudal to me. You're defined by someone else's version of the people you came from. It's an economically based version of 'I'm up, you're down.' "

He fell silent for a moment, then spoke. "It doesn't

matter anymore. That's one of the things I love about this city. It's this little peculiar oasis of meritocracy."

"Hoyt, you've got to be kidding. The 'who's on top' game is alive and well in the City of St. Francis. We have the power brokers and the social butterflies and the nouveau insanely rich geeks and nerds. You are so, so idealizing this city."

"I don't think so, Miss Maggie. You and I both know that those socialites can be tougher than nails. And what I love about them, and why I still take pride in this silly magazine, is that some of those social butterflies are perfectly willing to go to the mat to get things done."

"Okay, okay," I said. "And some of them are willing to get their lovely, manicured hands very dirty in doing actual manual labor."

"You're thinking of Grace Plummer. And I am so proud of the story we did on her."

"I am, too." We both paused for a moment, thinking of the glamorous Grace Plummer, who transformed herself and her life from a tragic childhood into a life of substantive, hard work.

"Spring and fall make me think of Grace," I said. "Sweating over a cultivator and digging amendments into the vegetable garden at A Mom's Place, and then harvesting good things to eat up until Thanksgiving."

"And outfitting all those sweet little unwed moms in her fancy dresses when they had a chance to go out and have fun."

Grace Plummer, murdered in the back of a limo, had prompted all of us to rethink what socially connected women could accomplish.

"Oh, my, we were snobs," I said. "Dismissive of

Grace without knowing all she had come from and all she had done."

"Hubris, Maggie, that's what it is."

"We're so entitled — after all, we are captains of a media empire."

Hoyt snorted. "Captains? Honey, we are foot soldiers in the rapidly disappearing world of flossy, glossy magazines. We are deckhands with slowly leaking life vests, and nothing more. We should be grateful for every day we miraculously stay in business."

"And if we're going to stay in business...."

"Oh, yes — what delightfully nefarious scheme do you have in mind for new revenue sources today?"

"I'm meeting with the TalkBack Foundation about their New American Journalism project."

"I smell a plot."

"Not a plot. An opportunity for mutual benefit. We need two interns for the summer, TalkBack wants to give these young wannabe media stars a chance for some practical work experience, and if all goes according to plan, these Genexters will be paid adequately, if not exactly handsomely, but with foundation dollars instead of *Small Town* dollars."

"And they all lived happily ever after," intoned Hoyt in his best bedtime-story voice.

"Correction: *We* all lived happily ever after. Or at least until the next 'sky-is-falling' prediction about the death of magazines."

"In all seriousness, Maggie," said Hoyt, "we're lucky you know how to pick the right pockets."

"I will take that as a compliment. Tell me what I should bring you from Oxford."

"Email me a picture of you at the Henhouse Museum."

"Better yet, I'll have Michael take a picture of Aunt Phoebe and Uncle Beau and me. Maybe in our going-to-the-Egg-Bowl regalia."

Hoyt laughed. "Pearls and all?"

"Pearls for me, rep tie for Michael. We'll fit in with the natives until one of us mouths off about politics or religion or the sanctity of the Maid of Cotton."

"Glad Michael's going with you," said Hoyt. "How's the domestic-bliss quotient Chez Fiori?"

"Is that code for something? Like am I behaving like the Whore of Babylon again?"

Hoyt patted my hand. "I believe that she was a metaphorical lady of easy virtue. Not a literal one."

"Biblically speaking, I am a pearl of great price these days. And besides, I'm too exhausted to get into any serious trouble. What with raising two boys, and being a captain of industry, and catering to every whim of Michael Fiori, tax superstar, constant reader of *The Leopard*, in Italian, I might add, and master of the kitchen."

"Cheer up," said Hoyt. "At least you're not married to one of those nitwit Southern gentlemen."

"Oh, no. No one ever called Michael a nitwit. That would be a dangerously foolish assumption. I mean it — what shall I bring you from Oxford?"

"Surprise me," said Hoyt.

CHAPTER 7

MAGGIE
OXFORD, MISSISSIPPI

"I love a road trip," I said to Michael.

He glanced over at me and grinned. "Me, too. Especially in a big-deal American car, no squabbling kids in the backseat, and an entire weekend of hearing Uncle Beau introduce me as 'Now, here's Maggie's Eye-Talian husband, all the way from California.'"

Michael's a changed man when it comes time to rent a car. Generally, he doesn't seem to care one way or another about automobiles, and in fact has promoted the purchase of matching Volvos every ten years or so, just to take one more shopping expedition off the agenda. Volvo dies? Buy another. But when he has the opportunity to rent something silly or outlandish, some primeval male energy seems to rear its priapic head. He looks for big cars with cushy backseats and retro brands — Cadillacs, Buicks, Oldsmobiles. "You know we don't have to resort to the backseat to make out anymore," I protest as I climb into a ginormous Lincoln and sink into the frontseat.

"Those were the days," he answered. "Just buckle up and let me know I'm going to get lucky tonight."

We had left the Memphis airport in early afternoon,

made a slight detour to the venerable Corky's for barbe-cue and artery-clogging, and now were winding south along Highway 55. The road took us past Hernando, Senatobia, Sardis (pop. 2,038 and home to the haunted hospital in North Panola County), and then a sharp left to turn east at Batesville to make our way to Oxford. When I was a kid, we'd stop in northern Mississippi to visit relatives in Water Valley, where generations of farmers, black and white, grow the sweetest water-melons on earth. When the boys are with us, we always have to stop and crack one open. I can still remember sitting on the folded-out tailgate when I was a kid with a lineup of cousins, all of us leaning out so we could spit seeds into the dirt at the side of the road.

"Seedless watermelons," I said. "What a dumb idea. Half the fun is spitting seeds."

"Well, I'm sure your uppity little heirloom nurs-ery can find you a vintage watermelon that will come replete with seeds," said Michael. "That way you can share your excellent spitting technique with the boys."

"Are you sorry they're not along?"

"Honestly? Not a bit. We pick the music, we pick the conversation topics, and we all get a little vacation from each other. Raising two boys is not always unmiti-gated pleasure. Besides, it gives Anya something to do." Anya, who had been our au pair when the boys were younger, had returned to Oakland to help out, now that she was in graduate school at Berkeley. Helping out, I feared, mostly meant indulging Zach and giving Josh way-too-good advice about being a hit with the ladies.

I felt my eyes fill. Michael glanced over at me. "Oh, cut it out, Maggie. You can't possibly start in on the 'one day they'll be gone away to school and we'll regret every minute we didn't have with them.' Think about dinner at City Grocery without having to mine the menu for something the little burger-and-sushi-heads will eat."

"I am not sentimental. I embrace the idea of dinner out with grown-ups. It's just...."

Michael sighed. "Don't think it escapes me that you pursued that whole innocent-guy-on-death-row thing because you were over-identifying with his mother and were envious of her jazz club."

I sat up straight. "I was not over-identifying; I just happened to like Ivory. Plus, who wouldn't be envious of owning a jazz club? Even the name of the club was cool — the Devil's Interval. I kept thinking one day Ivory might invite me to sing at the Devil's Interval."

"That would be interesting. I didn't think you sang outside the shower and the whole canon of 'Itsy-Bitsy Spider' and 'One Hundred Bottles of Beer on the Wall.'"

"Well, okay, not sing. But maybe I could just get on a slinky dress and lounge on the piano."

Michael reached over to pat my knee. "We all need a dream, *cara*."

CHAPTER 8

MAGGIE
OXFORD

William Faulkner lived here. When I was a kid coming to visit my mom's family in Oxford, my literature-loving parents, Isabella and Fred, would take us out to Rowan Oak to see Mr. Faulkner's Greek Revival house. Because my parents didn't believe in censoring anything we wanted to read, I remember puzzling through *As I Lay Dying* at about age ten, trying to figure out where the punctuation went and why. "Sin and love and fear are just sounds that people who never sinned or loved or feared have for what they never had and cannot have until they forget the words," I declaimed.

"Here we go," said Michael. "Faulkner, right? I always feel as if he's the uninvited guest in the car on this drive."

"I invite him! You know, he knew my grandmother, Alma."

"I know," said Michael. "He admired her red hair."

I laughed. "So you do listen to these stories from time to time."

"Indeed I do."

And there just before us was the square. "I'm assuming," said Michael, driving slowly past Neilson's department store, Square Books, a bronze William Faulkner, pipe in hand, contemplating the city square, and City Grocery, where last time we dined, two of the famous Manning gentlemen — Archie and Eli — were sitting at the next table, "that we'll go directly to Phoebe and Beau's?"

"I guess so," I said, looking longingly at Square Books, the storybook version of an independent American bookstore, opened by Richard and Lisa Howorth in 1979 and still the platinum standard for true book lovers. Wood floors, strong coffee, and an upstairs balcony when you've found your book and just need to sit down and dive right in.

"Earth to Maggie," called Michael. "Next stop, Phoebe and Beau's and a tall, cold Abita. We'll walk over to the bookstore later."

In the way of small towns, Oxford didn't exactly embrace Mr. Faulkner in his lifetime. "Count No-Count," they called him, since he felt little but contempt for a salaryman's life. Now, of course, Oxford has bragging rights about its status as keeper of the not-too-shabby Mississippi literary flame, from Eudora Welty and Walker Percy on through to Willie Morris, Donna Tartt, and, yep, a pretty good storyteller, John Grisham. But Mr. Faulkner, now, he trumps them all.

CHAPTER 9

VICTORIA'S JOURNAL, 1863

*"Stranger! if you, passing, meet me, and desire to speak to
me, why should you not speak to me?/And why should I
not speak to you?"*

— Walt Whitman

Walter paid me a high compliment this evening. "Miss Victoria," he said to his Quaker friend Levi Coffin, known to
his admirers as the President of the Underground Railroad,
"is a secret-keeper. You can trust her word. We met on a
train from Washington, DC, to Richmond, Virginia, and
have been friends ever since.

"As you know," he added, "I do not hold with this nonsense of people needing to be introduced. Miss Victoria
and I kept each other in high spirits on a tedious journey."

I find it amusing that Walter pays attention to secret-keeping among others. He surely cannot have many secrets
left to tell, because he talks and talks and talks about every
thought and then pours those thoughts directly onto the
page and then ceaselessly arranges and rearranges them.
Hence, his masterwork — *Leaves of Grass* — is as change-

able as the weather. Of course, Walter is correct: I do keep
information to myself. I like to think of myself as a brave
woman, but I am not a brave fool.

"Miss Victoria," said Mr. Coffin, "I wish we had your
discretion and your talent during the height of our Underground Railroad days." He sighed. "Pretty young
women were among our most successful conductors and
stationmasters."

"Ah, now," said Walter, "I am not sure I would settle on
so poor a word as 'pretty' for our Victoria."

I felt my cheeks color. "Walter," I said, "I will accept Mr.
Coffin's compliment with thanks and put an end to that
discussion. Instead, let us talk of more interesting things. I
would welcome the opportunity to learn more about how
the railroad worked. It seems like magic to me, transform-
ing enslaved human beings into free men and women."

But Walter was not to be distracted. "Handsome," he
said. "Striking, with all that glorious mass of red — no, not
red, say, rather, blood-red, carmine, copper, russet, deep
mahogany." He stopped, and looked up at the ceiling, puff-
ing on his pipe and contemplating the low, smoke-dark-
ened ceiling of the inn.

Mr. Coffin and I exchanged glances. "Walter, my
friend," said Mr. Coffin, "you are embarrassing this innocent young woman."

Walter looked astonished. "Embarrassing her? She is
fearless, she is outspoken — believe me sir, you do not
want to get on her bad side. She can be a heartless but

very effective nurse, I have seen this with my own eyes. She will wheedle and cajole and lecture and threaten some poor wounded soul, imprisoned in his hospital bed, until he begins making the progress Miss Victoria wishes to see."

"Nonetheless," said Mr. Coffin, "I would like to know a little more about Miss Cardworthy."

"I, for one, am weary of this subject, sir," I said. "But I am happy to answer your questions, if I am able."

"Well, then, let us start with the most obvious question: How is it that a lovely young Southern woman is tending wounded Yankees?"

"I am agnostic on the topic of color," I said. "Wounded men are wounded men, in blue or in gray."

"It took Victoria some time to share this information with me," said Walter. "But she began her work as a nurse at Chimborazo, that great, sprawling hospital that takes in the Confederates. And then —" Walter paused for dramatic effect "— she crossed over. She put herself on the train from Richmond to Washington and is now a stalwart at the Armory and other Union hospitals. And," he added, miming the tip of a hat, "she does what many are not willing to do. She cares for the Union's dark soldiers as well."

Mr. Coffin surveyed me with new interest. "Negro soldiers?" he said.

"As I said, sir, I do not see color as a differentiator of great interest."

Mr. Coffin shook his head, "Oh, my dear. That is why I am an abolitionist. Sadly, color is a shocking, murderous differentiator."

I nodded. "Yes, I understand what you are saying. And I commend and admire you for your work. But we are so very far away from the day when color is not the first thing people observe. So, in the meantime, my small part is simply not seeing it at all."

"May I ask," said Mr. Coffin, "how you came to have such independent ideas? Perhaps your parents were free-thinkers or Transcendentalists, like Walter's friend Ralph Waldo Emerson?"

"Ha!" said Walter. "You're on the wrong path, my friend."

"My parents are kind and generous people," I said. "And my father, in particular, did want me to understand the wider world. When I was still a girl, he took me to New York to hear Elizabeth Blackwell speak. She was a wonder to me, speaking frankly about how she had earned a medical degree, even though no other woman had ever been admitted to an American medical school. It was very difficult to listen to her and not think — 'why can't I be useful as well?' "

"Ah, Dr. Blackwell," said Mr. Coffin. "She helped gather many of us together at the Cooper Institute in New York just as this terrible war began. So compelling was her leadership that men and women alike worked together with one goal, to form the Women's Central Relief Association so that the work of many smaller groups could coalesce and be more effective."

"More to admire," I said. "I know that her work turned into the United States Sanitary Commission, caring for sick and injured soldiers. It is a group whose work I respect very much."

Walter stood to stir up the fire, poking vigorously at the disappearing logs, so that a wave of wood smoke drifted our way.

"Easy, my friend," said Mr. Coffin. "You will choke the very breath out of all of us."

"Now," said Walter, "there is more to Miss Victoria's extreme notions. She is also, like many of your seditious comrades, an advocate for the rights of women."

"Ah," said Mr. Coffin. "She should meet our mutual friend Lucretia Mott."

"I have had the privilege of hearing Miss Mott speak," I said. "She stirs the soul as vigorously as Walter stirs the fire."

Mr. Coffin threw back his head and laughed. "But there's a difference, Miss Victoria — Walter clouds the air with smoke and soot, and I would say that Miss Mott seeks simply to clear the air."

Something lightened in that very moment in Walter's cluttered, anything-but-tidy attic room at 456 Sixth Street West. We had all spoken our minds without fear. It was as if we were peers, speaking safely in that dimly lit circle around the fire.

Mr. Coffin picked up his jar of lemonade and took a hearty swallow.

"What do you think of that refreshment, dear Levi?"

Walter asked.

"Like all your refreshments, my friend, it is quite dreadful, but I appreciate the hospitality nonetheless. Now how is it, Miss Victoria, that you have come to have such advanced views on race, considering your upbringing in our Southern states?"

"Although slavery first set its evil roots in the South," I said, "there is precious little difference in the attitudes of Southerners and Northerners. The great majority of Northerners fear, subjugate, and exploit the darker races in nearly precisely the way our Southern friends do. I have no doubt that if a Grand Prince of India landed on our shores, he would have a lonely time of it finding welcome in Charlotte or Chicago."

"Yes, but —"

I raised my hand to silence Mr. Coffin. "We have no need of argument, Mr. Coffin. I believe we share the same values. Human beings should be free souls — to make their way in the world, to raise their families, to do God's work."

"Whoever She may be!" announced Walter. Mr. Coffin chuckled.

"I do not yet believe that it is possible God is a woman," I said, and there was ice in my voice. "No woman would allow the forcible separation of husband and wife, or parent and child."

The room grew quiet. I saw Walter and Mr. Coffin exchange glances. I had seen such glances before. They thought we were having a cordial, lively conversation, and

I had spoilt the milk by responding so fiercely. I stood. "I will bid you good evening, gentlemen. I am sorry I have taken the bloom off this pleasant gathering."

Mr. Coffin leapt to his feet. "No, no, my dear. We did not mean to take what you are saying lightly. And I assure you that you have friends in the world who share your point of view about the rights of women. It's just that...."

I looked him in the eye. "It's just that we can only fight one battle at a time. Is that not right? And abolition must come first."

Walter shook his head. "I am a poet and a nurse, my dear. We agree on so much. But slavery is anathema to this great nation of ours. And this is the battle we must win immediately. You, of all people, have seen what combat can do to the beautiful human form and human spirit."

He reached out his hand to me. I looked at this very odd, completely fearless, no-longer-young man, and I had to relent. "You are right, sir. We have our priorities. We are friends and we must allow for differences of opinion."

We shook hands all around, and settled back into our places. "But..." I said, and Mr. Coffin and Walter began to laugh.

"Once more into the fray," said Walter.

"But," I said, raising my voice, "when it is time to fight for the rights of our sisters, and not just our brothers, I will look to you for support and advocacy."

And there, in that dim room, they agreed. In later years, Walter swore I had bound him with a devil's pact, one he could not escape. I could not help but laugh, but I, too, felt that we had made an unbreakable promise to each another.

I walked home alone, despite their protests, back to the rooming-house where we ladies of questionable repute took refuge. Nurses were little better than fallen women. We had seen and touched the bodies of men. We had washed unspeakable things from the skin of perfect strangers. We had heard their secrets and their confessions. We had seen them weep and beg for death.

No one should see such things, least of all those fragile creatures known as women.

The gaslights lit my path from Walter's room at the inn back to the rooming-house Mrs. Marshall kept. She, too, kept her own counsel, but she claimed to admire the work we nurses undertook, and she regularly walked over to Campbell Hospital when her peaches and plums ripened, delivering fresh fruit to the hospital. She would never come in. She would simply leave her sacks of sweet fruit on the front step and hurry away.

When I reached her door, I knocked for entry. Her houseman, Raphael, let me in. "Welcome home, Miss Victoria," he said. "You had a caller this evening, but I told him I thought you might be late coming home."

"Did you get his name, Raphael?" I asked, untying my bonnet ribbons and tidying my hair.

He shook his head. "No, and he did not leave a card. But he said he would call tomorrow." He hesitated. "And he said one more thing. He mentioned that he was looking forward to seeing your scarlet curls and hearing your conversation."

I smiled. "Thank you, Raphael. I believe he is an old… friend. And I will be glad to see him." I started up the stairs, suddenly longing for my bed and a long, sweet, dreamless sleep. I knew who was coming and what he would want. And I would need every ounce of my strength.

CHAPTER 10

MAGGIE
OXFORD

While "meat and two sides" might be standard Southern parlance, no self-respecting member of my family would be satisfied with anything less than three, four, or maybe five sides.

I surveyed Aunt Phoebe's company table. It had looked like a magazine cover when we began our supper — golden, fragrant fried chicken, a little fried catfish just in case someone wanted that plus the chicken. And the sides: potato salad, coleslaw with peanuts, okra, black-eyed peas, a dish of homemade pickles. Iced sweet tea for Phoebe and me, and a couple of Louisiana-brewed Abitas for the gentlemen.

Gradually, the table grew quiet, as three of the four of us were reduced to near stupor. Aunt Phoebe was still jumping up every five minutes to bring just one more thing: corn sticks, accompanied by honey from Uncle Beau's hive, and of course, a big bowl of the twenty-four-hour fruit salad my mother makes — hand-pitted bing cherries, almonds, marshmallows. How exactly is it that any Southerners live past forty? But there was Phoebe, maybe 110 pounds, in her spotless, pressed linen dress, just nibbling and hopping up and down to ferry still more food to the table.

"Now, for dessert," she began, "I've made pecan pie for Maggie and banana cream for Michael, and oh, my neighbor sent over some homemade pralines."

Michael put both hands up in the air. Phoebe stopped in her tracks, "Michael, honey, what's wrong? Are you choking?"

"Phoebe," he said, "I am surrendering. I beg you, can we have a timeout before dessert?"

"The Henhouse Museum!" I said. "Let's take a little walkabout and get the highlights tour."

"That is a fine idea," said Beau. "And since we are putting you two lovebirds in the henhouse guest suite, we can get you all moved in."

At three in the morning, I startled myself — and Michael — out of a dead sleep. Michael rolled over and looked at me. "*Cara*, what's wrong? What are you talking about? It's the middle of the night."

I shook my head. "I was talking? What was I saying?"

He pulled me close. "Beats me. I'm just a guy trying to sleep. Whatever it was, you can tell me in the morning." He pulled me close, tugged the covers up over my shoulders, and was snoring rhythmically in under a minute. I stared at the wall. Just above the dresser hung the twin to the daguerreotype Phoebe had sent me. My doppelganger looked back at me.

"Hello," I whispered. "I think I was talking to you, Victoria. And maybe you were talking back." The room was silent. The window shade moved in the dark, and a familiar fragrance blew through the room. It couldn't be lilac; spring was long gone. I wiggled out from under Michael's arm and crept over to the window. I lifted

the shade and leaned onto the window sill. Right outside the window, the top branches of witch hazel shrubs
brushed against the sill. I reached out, broke off a small
piece, heavy with yellow flowers, and brought it close to
my face. "When lilacs last in the dooryard bloomed..."
I whispered. But I must have been half dreaming, because it was far too late for lilacs. I tiptoed back to bed.
Victoria and I exchanged glances, or at least that's how
it felt. She looked brave, confident, strong on that six-
teen-hand-high horse. "Tell me your secrets," I said.
And then I fell back asleep.

CHAPTER 11

MAGGIE
OXFORD

Over breakfast — mercifully we got away with yogurt and fruit — Aunt Phoebe outlined the day. "Now, you children can just take it easy this morning. Beau's already headed out on his rounds, but he left early so he should be back in plenty of time for the Egg Bowl. I'll just finish up in my office."

Phoebe's office was, of course, the kitchen, a picture-perfect homage to the 1950s, with an elderly but pristine Wedgwood stove, a dishwasher that was so noisy when it was turned on it sounded as if a family of beavers were inside gnawing specks off the dinnerware, and a long, sunny window hung with starched dotted swiss café curtains. Phoebe's "office" was a long-running joke her children had started when they were small and their mama would tell them to play nice so she could "finish up." Since Phoebe was always cooking or baking or canning or preserving, there was no finishing up, as far as I could tell. There was just cleaning up from one project to get ready for the next. Beau used to say, "You children leave your mama alone — she's got work to do in her office."

Michael and I exchanged looks and tossed a coin to

see who would pursue the futile effort to help Phoebe with her myriad chores. I lost, so I strolled purposefully into the kitchen and plucked an ironed apron off Phoebe's antique coat rack. I tied the apron strings around twice and said, "Phoebe, I'm wearing an apron, so you've got to give me a job to do."

She glanced at her watch and back at me. I could tell she was considering a big move. "You know what, darlin'? If we're going to get an early start for the picnic tables, you could do a little job or two for me."

"Hallelujah!" I said. "Bring 'em on."

In a few minutes, and with just about twice as many detailed instructions as any idiot would receive, but especially a Yankee idiot would need, Phoebe had briefed me on my two assignments: stuffing the hard-boiled eggs she'd probably prepared in the dead of night while we mere mortals slept, and garnishing each one with a sliver of Kalamata olive — or as Phoebe called them, "calamity" olives. I stood at the world's most ancient cutting board and meticulously slivered each calamity.

"You know, Phoebe," I ventured. "You can buy Kalamata olives already slivered."

"Oh, I know. I've seen them in the fancy shelves at the Piggly Wiggly. For you working gals, timesavers like that are just more precious than rubies. But I think about all those slivers sitting in that olive juice with all the flavor leaching out — because once you slice them, they're just not the same." I pondered as I slivered. I wasn't too sure about the science behind Phoebe's theory, but she could be right. And no one's deviled eggs tasted as good as hers. Besides, what higher calling did I have than standing in an operating room/clean kitchen and slivering away?

"Phoebe, we loved staying in the henhouse last night. You know, the only time Michael ever experiences ironed sheets is at your house. He asked me this morning if you'd be willing to fly out to California once a week and iron ours?"

She was quiet for a moment. "You know, Maggie, you could wash a few sets and send them to me and I'd iron them and send them back? We could get a little backlog in your linen closet so Michael would always have pressed sheets. People sleep better on ironed sheets, that's what I believe."

I put my knife down. "Phoebe, you know I'm teasing you, right?"

She frowned over some unseen flaw in her coconut cake, wielding the icing spatula like a perfectionist neurosurgeon. She looked up. "Oh, honey, you are always joking. I can't always tell when you're serious — but anyway, you know that one of your cousin Betty's boys is working at FedEx. I bet he could get us a discount on sending those sheets."

"Phoebe, you missed your calling. You ought to run logistics for the military."

"You just watch yourself, Missy. You keep an eye on that knife and those calamities — we don't have time for a stop at the ER on our way to the game."

"Plus," I offered, "we'd have to rinse all the blood off the olives, and that would really throw us off schedule." Phoebe tsk-tsked at me.

We fell back into a companionable silence.

"I have so many questions about all those things in the henhouse," I finally said. "I hardly know where to start. Does Beau know the names of all the people in those photos?"

"Lots of them. Not all, but you know he's a very persistent fellow, so if you turn up something you want to know, he'll figure it out."

I thought about all the things I'd seen in our first stroll through the henhouse: photos (loose, framed, and enclosed in albums), paintings, sketches, boxes of carefully filed newspaper clippings, and family Bibles, including two inscribed to my grandmother, Alma. The first was a white leather book with gold-edged pages, a classic St. James version containing the Old and New Testaments. On the flyleaf it read:

On the occasion of your marriage to Morris Stern, September 18, 1947. God has kept you safe, now Morris will keep you happy.

Your loving Mother and Father

The second was a soft, cloth-bound Torah, with Papa Morris's quick strokes on the first page:

You, my darling Alma, are a price above rubies. When we are together, I fear no serpent in our garden.

With all my heart and soul, your Morris

"What Great-Grandmother Jessamyn wrote to Alma, what Morris wrote to Alma — those were such elegant, heartfelt thoughts," I said. " 'I fear no serpent in our garden' — can you imagine emailing something like that?"

"I can," said Phoebe. "You have written me beautiful emails. And when they are very special, I print them out and I put them in one of your grandmother Alma's hatboxes."

I shook my head. "Really? I think my emails are all about trolling for family gossip — which you, of course, being so kind-hearted, refuse to divulge — or asking you to re-send me one of your recipes I've lost yet again."

"You quoted some poem to me that just filled my heart when my friend Sarah died." Phoebe wiped her hands on the dishtowel. "I learned it by heart." Standing straight, with her hands folded in front of her like a schoolgirl, she recited:

"Death is nothing at all. It does not count. I have only slipped away into the next room. Nothing has happened. Everything remains exactly as it was. I am I, and you are you, and the old life that we lived so fondly together is untouched, unchanged. Whatever we were to each other, that we are still. Call me by the old familiar name. Speak of me in the easy way which you always used. Put no difference into your tone. Wear no forced air of solemnity or sorrow. Laugh as we always laughed at the little jokes that we enjoyed together. Play, smile, think of me, pray for me."

Phoebe dabbed at her eyes with the corner of the dishtowel.

"You know, that's not exactly a poem," I said. "It's from a sermon that Canon Henry Scott Holland preached at St. Paul's in London. He gave that sermon in 1910, and he died in 1918, six months before the armistice."

"The eleventh hour of the eleventh day of the eleventh month," said Phoebe. "My father taught us that. It was such a horrific war."

"They're all horrific. But I've always wondered about Canon Holland — his happy-talk beliefs about death must have been tested before he died."

Phoebe looked at me sharply. "I didn't think that was happy talk, Maggie. It broke my heart when my friend Sarah died. We used to talk every Sunday afternoon on the phone, three o'clock in the afternoon on the dot, her time in Connecticut, two o'clock my time. And after you wrote to me, I realized I could still talk to her. So I take myself for a walk on Sunday afternoons and I tell Sarah what's been going on, and if I'm bothered about something, I just yak, yak, yak, and I can almost hear her answers." Phoebe began stacking her trademark tower o' Tupperware to pack into the picnic baskets. "Just so you know, Maggie, your Mr. Holland's comments comforted me greatly, so I'll thank you not to disrespect them as 'happy talk.' "

Good work, Maggie, I thought. Being snarky to the nicest person on the planet. I put my slivering instrument down and wrapped my arms around Phoebe's shoulders. "I am an awful smart-mouth, Aunt Phoebe. I am so sorry."

She patted my cheek. "Honey, you always had a bit of a sassy mouth. I wouldn't know you otherwise."

"Last night —" I said, stopping.

"Pardon?"

"Last night, I woke up at three in the morning, and I must have awakened Michael, because he asked me who I'd been talking to. I had the oddest feeling I'd fallen asleep looking at the old photo of Victoria, and I was talking to her."

"In the same room, darlin'."

The eggs were done, each one stuffed and bedecked with one infinitesimal olive sliver, packed carefully in — what else — a deviled egg platter, which she lowered like a priceless piece of art into a sturdy Tupperware container. While I had labored over those eggs, Phoebe had efficiently packed two picnic baskets with chicken salad, roasted zucchini, peppers, and sweet onions from her garden, spoonbread, and a cherry pie. Uncle Beau was rattling around with two wagons, Radio Flyers that had belonged to their kids (aka my cousins) and now repurposed for tailgating afternoons. A cooler with ice, wine, and beer perched on one wagon. Uncle Beau hoisted the picnic baskets, batting away offers of help. "Now, honey, you know we don't want our ladies to get all smudged and perspire-y from heavy lifting."

I gave up, though I had seen Phoebe out in the garden since I was a little girl, attacking a non-performing plant with a hoe and a shovel, relentless until she had upended some strong-rooted plant, either to consign it to the compost heap or to replant it in a more favorable location. Phoebe caught my eye and placed her finger on her lips. "They have to believe what they have to believe," she whispered.

Owing to my not-yet-advanced age, Uncle Beau did permit me to pull the lighter of the wagons, heading across the square and off into Hollingsworth Field.

Football day in Oxford always looks like a wedding reception to me. Ladies in pearls, gentlemen in khaki slacks and blue blazers. In recent years, the ties had been dwindling, but a stalwart few still dressed like gentlemen. Uncle Beau, of course, was turned out in a crisp white shirt and a striped rep tie.

Our little procession's ranks swelled as we moved across the square: cousins — actual and honorary — families, pretty college girls in linens and pearls, a marching band playing (of course) "Dixie," and the usual conglomerate of kids too young to embrace the culture and old stiff-legged guys who'd raise a glass to toast the "Speed Limit 18" sign on campus, the insiders' homage to number eighteen, the one, the only Archie Manning.

We turned the corner into the Grove, and every single childhood memory about Saturday afternoons and Ole Miss football came back to me. The air was already alive with

Hotty Toddy, Hotty Toddy, Gosh Almighty!
Who the Hell Are We? Hey!
Flim Flam, Bim Bam
Ole Miss by Damn!

"Tailgate time," called Beau, leading the way through the sea of popup tents to find the one he'd reserved for us.

The sophomore who was officially saving our place waved an Ole Miss pennant. "Over here, Mr. Beau!"

Phoebe waved back, greeted the young man with a hug, and said, "Marcus, say hello to our niece, Maggie Fiori, and her husband, Michael. This is Marcus, and he is in pre-med and is going to go into the business of saving lives. And I can't wait till he's out of school and will be my doctor so I can let poor Doc Harry retire!"

We shook hands. "That is some endorsement," I said.

Marcus grinned and leaned in close. "I think she's

just encouraging me. Doc Harry treats her like the Queen of Sheba. She'll never let him retire."

Meanwhile, Beau had shucked his seersucker blazer and, with Michael and Marcus's help, began setting up the ancient folding picnic table. In an instant it was covered with a good white cloth, red-checked napkins, and an ocean of Tupperware containers. Phoebe presented Marcus with his own container. "I wish you'd stay and eat with us," she said, "but I know you want to go visit with your friends. So here's a little collection of nibbles for you and that pretty girl I hear you're seeing."

Marcus looked startled. Beau laughed, "Marcus, my boy, if you don't know Oxford is a small town by now, you're never gonna learn. You could learn some diagnostic skills from Phoebe — she can spot a man with a fatal condition, otherwise known as love, at one hundred paces." Marcus blushed, shook hands all around, and gratefully escaped, Tupperware in hand.

"Let's sit down," said Phoebe, "before the hot stuff gets cold and the cold stuff gets warm."

"To feast and friends," said Uncle Beau. "And may the best Rebs win."

"Doesn't matter," said Phoebe. "You know what we say around here — Ole Miss may not win the game, but we will always win the party."

CHAPTER 12

VICTORIA'S JOURNAL, 1862
RICHMOND, VIRGINIA

> *"I employed every capacity with which God has endowed
> me, and the result was far more successful than my hopes
> could have flattered me to expect."*
>
> — Rose O'Neal Greenhow

By nine the morning after my visit with Walter and Mr.
Coffin, I had washed, dressed, and breakfasted. I wanted
to be prepared when my visitor came to call, and nothing
sustains a person's character like a hearty morning meal. I
was expected at the hospital that afternoon, and my visitor,
I felt sure, knew every detail of my schedule.

At 9:15, there was a rap on my door. Raphael said,
"Miss Victoria, your caller has returned. He's waiting for
you on the front porch."

I picked up my bonnet and opened the door. Raphael
looked over his shoulder as if expecting the enemy com-
batants to come right up the stairs to my room. "And Miss
Victoria…" He lowered his voice. "He still declined to give
me his name."

"It's all right," I said. "Maybe our mystery caller is bringing me a surprise."

On the porch, a tall man took his ease, his hat in his hand. He surveyed the street as if he was the proprietor of every square inch — every house, the blacksmith's forge, the wagons rolling by, and perhaps every man and woman, black or white or some shade in between, who walked by. I knew he heard my step behind him, but he didn't turn around until I spoke.

"Hello, Eli. How kind of you to pay a call. What an... expected surprise."

At that he turned, reached out his hand to grasp mine, drew me a little too close, bent with a grand flourish, paused, and then deliberately turned my hand palm side up and grazed his lips lightly upon it. He stepped back and breathed in. "Vic, my dear, you must be the only nurse in this infernal war whose hand always smells like crushed lavender. What do you do to get rid of the smell of lye and laudanum?"

I withdrew my hand. "And you, sir, are not the only miscreant who masquerades so poorly as a gentleman." I gestured at the slope-backed chairs on the porch. "May I invite you to take a seat and state your business with me?"

"My business?" he said. "I would think that old friends simply might get together to reminisce about our childhood days."

"Eli, most of the things I remember about our childhood involve you getting me into some scrape or another — building a fort and then burning it down, nearly setting

fire to my parents' house in the process. Or, you wanting
to 'practice' your kissing technique and using me as your
practice dummy. Remember how my father caught us and
I was sent to my room for a week? And may I add, you had
three years on me, and used those to excellent advantage."

Eli looked upward and smiled. "This is how men and
women differ. I have such positive memories of our adventures together. And I would like to remind you that I
walked you home from the schoolhouse to keep the rowdy
boys away. Remember that? And you and I would make up
silly songs all the way to your house."

As usual, Eli was breaking down my resolve to not get
into more mischief. I said, "Here's the one I remember —
you made this one up, so of course, you were the hero of
the song:

" 'Vic and Eli went down to the creek, Vic's little boat
sprang a big old leak; Oh no, said Vic, our outlook is bleak;
All right, said Eli, I'll take a peek....' "

"I don't remember what comes next," said Eli.

"Oh, yes, you do. The rest of it was variations on all the
parts of me you'd take a peek at!"

"I miss those days," he said, reaching for my hand.

I placed his hand back in his lap. "Very well, Eli, I will
repeat my original request — state your business and be
off with you!"

"I have a counter-offer, Vic, and it involves a stroll
this lovely morning and paying a call on someone I'd like
you to meet." He gestured toward the porch stairs leading

down to the packed dirt road. "Shall we?"

We looked at each other, each waiting for the other to blink. "I trust," said Eli, "that your brother has returned to good health. Nothing like the care of an excellent nurse and good food and drink to speed a convalescent's progress."

I shook my head. "Eli, does it ever concern you that every human transaction you carry out, even those that seem so benevolent on first blush, all involve keeping accounts? This has been the case since we were schoolchildren together, and you would barter a peppermint for a kiss."

Unfazed, Eli said, "Those were the days when you were willing to barter, Vic. Now, we're both adults, and I hope that you will credit me as a man who is always delighted to do a good turn. You saved your brother's life, of that I have no doubt. But if you give a man something to look forward to — a good meal, a decent bottle of whiskey — I think that simply fuels the good flame of recovery. It was my honor to be helpful in some small way to your family."

I lifted my index finger to my mouth, gave it one good lick, and made a tally gesture in the air that could not have been misunderstood. Eli knew I was calling him on the endless, rarely legal, barely ethical rounds of give-and-take he pursued.

"You wound me, Victoria."

"Indeed. You and I have been keeping score since we were in Miz Lizzie's one-room schoolhouse in Oxford. But thank you for your inquiries about my brother. Jeremiah is back at work on the farm, and though the loss of a leg is a terrible thing for a man who makes his living with hard, physical labor, he is finding ways to keep the farm running with help from neighbors, and of course from his beloved, Elizabeth."

"Ah," said Eli. "So they are sticking together? That takes some grit, to fall in love with a whole man and then marry a...broken one."

"They are being married this fall, and I assure you that Elizabeth sees Jeremiah as an entirely whole man." I felt the color rising in my cheeks. "Have you ever been in love, Eli? Or perhaps, I should ask, has anyone ever been in love with you?"

Eli shook his head, and put his hand to his heart, all melodrama, and if my suspicions were true, there was not a sincere bone in his body. "Again you misjudge me, dear Victoria. And I assure you that many, many young ladies have found me...well, certainly not repugnant. But, sadly, I have only been in love once, and so I must take my pleasure in admiring relationships that people such as your brother and Elizabeth have established. Believe me when I tell you, I wish them every blessing."

"Thank you," I said. "And now, perhaps you'd like to tell me what you came to ask."

"Nothing onerous."

"Or illegal? Or unethical? Or indefensible?"

"Not at all. Well, not really."

"Hmmm. Here it comes."

"I simply want you to accompany me to meet with a

friend and her daughter who have fallen on hard times."

I raised an eyebrow. "And how wonderful to find you helping those less fortunate than yourself. Who are these people who merit your attention and...kindness?"

"Mrs. Rose Greenhow and her daughter, Little Rose. Perhaps you know of her?"

"Rose Greenhow? The notorious Rose Greenhow? When you say she and her daughter have fallen on hard times, what you mean is, she's going to jail. I heard that the powers-that-be are shutting down Fort Greenhow, and Mrs. Greenhow is going to be in residence at the Old Capitol Prison."

Rose Greenhow, who was connected to everyone from Dolley Madison to Stephen Douglas, had become ever more outspoken in her Confederate sympathies. And while her many protectors and advocates had shielded her from the harshest consequences of her transgressions by arranging for house arrest at the *soi-disant* Fort Greenhow, news in the gossipy small town of Washington, DC, was that Rose's kid-glove treatment was drawing to a close.

"You are well informed," said Eli. "But I would have expected no less."

"I am sorry for Mrs. Greenhow and her youngest daughter, but I cannot see how I can be of service to them."

"Ah, perhaps I was not clear. I believe Mrs. Greenhow can be of service to us. I have taken the liberty of booking seats on the afternoon train from Richmond to Washington. We can visit with Mrs. Greenhow there before...."

"Before she's locked up and better supervised than she is now," I interrupted. "And why would she want to see me?"

"Because she knows that you, in fact, come from a Confederacy family."

"I have made no secret of that."

"Just so. I think it would be helpful to Mrs. Greenhow to have a sympathetic listener about her...activities."

Without speaking, I put on my bonnet, tied the ribbons with a determined yank, and set off down the porch steps and onto the road. Eli watched for a few moments and then strode down the stairs and up the road to catch me. "Don't be a fool, Vic. This is a rare opportunity. Mrs. Greenhow is chafing at the increasing restrictions on her visitors, and she will be happy to see you."

"Setting aside why I would want to see her, I'm not sure her jailers, even the more lenient ones at Ft. Greenhow, would be happy to see someone associated with the Confederacy paying a call on Mrs. Greenhow."

"That's where you're wrong, Vic. I have already discussed a potential visit with the lieutenant in charge of all the spying ladies at Fort Greenhow. You would be most welcome. You walked away from your Confederate ties, and your reputation for caring for the wounded, blue or gray, makes you above reproach."

We continued walking, and I loosened my bonnet strings. Either Eli was giving me a headache, as he so often did, or I had tied everything too tightly. Perhaps both.

"Lest you forget, Eli, I am still employed at the Chimborazo Hospital, which is, at last glance, a Confederate hospital."

"Oh, Vic, everyone knows you care for anyone who needs it: Union, Confederate, colored, white."

"Everyone, Eli? I find it highly unlikely that everyone is aware of the sympathies and values of one nurse among many."

Eli smiled. "As ever, Vic, you minimize your reputation. The fact that you still have a horse, that you move freely between Chimborazo and the Armory hospitals, makes you something of a unique personage."

"I visit the Armory to learn new techniques and to visit my friends there," I protested.

"So you say. Remember you and I have known each other since childhood. And so you cannot bluff and evade with me. I know what a facile story-spinner you are. And that's precisely why I think you and Mrs. Greenhow will enjoy each other's company."

"And my plan in pursuing this visit? Besides the milk of human kindness that flows in my veins? Truly, what is it you think I can gain from this visit?"

"You are such a well-read young woman, Victoria. I am sure you know the play by Mr. Richard Brinsley Sheridan, *The School for Scandal?*"

" 'A school for scandal!/tell me I beseech you,/Needs there a School this modish art to teach you?' "

Eli shook his head. "Ah, Victoria, you manage to amaze

and irk me, all at the same time."

"First performed," I continued, "in 1777 at the Drury Lane Theatre, a place I long to visit one day."

"It will be my pleasure to take you there when we have the leisure to make future plans. But today, I entreat you to visit Mrs. Greenhow. We are pursuing a school of an entirely different kind. And I think you may be precisely the person to help lead this endeavor."

It is foolish to ask a question when one already knows the answer, but I could not resist. "A school not of scandal, but of spies. Is that it, Eli?"

CHAPTER 13

VICTORIA'S JOURNAL, 1862
RICHMOND, VIRGINIA

In the end, of course, I agreed to Eli's plan. He is a man of great persuasive powers, and not all of them involve manipulation, blackmail, and horse-trading. Literally, horse-trading, because I know that Eli engaged in elaborate wheeling and dealing to keep my beloved horse, Courage, in my care. After I had agreed to hospital work, rather than my itinerant nurse-on-horseback rides from battlefield to battlefield, there was no compelling reason that I still needed Courage for my own. Horses were dearer than gold, as conscription on both sides gathered and consumed both soldiers and their mounts.

Somehow, Eli managed to negotiate an exception for Courage, and I was deeply grateful. It wasn't just that I thought of Courage as my partner in my work or that we'd been together since I was a girl; somehow he was also my getaway plan. Since I learned to walk, I have abhorred feeling trapped. My poor parents! They were always calling for me. "Victoria, where are you?" I would wander off the farm and into the woods, and it is likely a miracle I survived to adulthood. But there are so many restrictions on the way we women can live our lives: what we can say, where we can walk, how we should dress, how we do or do not have access to money we earn. I am cursed with an intemperate tongue and a short temper, and knowing that I can saddle Courage, ride as well as any man, and be off, just like that, often kept me from straying more visibly, more spectacularly away from societal norms. Or at least it did for a while.

And now Eli had woven another spider web to entrap me, and knowing full well that I would probably live to regret it, I agreed to meet with Mrs. Greenhow. Was she a spy? Oh, yes. And a highly skilled one. Her tongue was as silver and sophisticated as mine was hasty and sharp. She was a woman of elegance, refinement, and, most of all, a sly sense of fun. Life was a social whirl at Mrs. Greenhow's. Despite the shortage of food and drink in the shops, good food and wine somehow miraculously appeared out of nowhere at her home, until it was converted to a temporary prison. Conversations danced around her parlor, pirouetting from local news to speculation to whispered contraband subjects. There was much laughter during a visit with Mrs. Greenhow, I had heard, and I believe she was an accomplished flirt and a highly successful extractor of information. The stories declare that by the end of an evening, Mrs. Greenhow went to bed with an ever-growing cache of information, and she was prepared to share it immediately with her most-favored Confederate officers.

Not for Rose Greenhow was the quick temper of Belle Boyd, who famously shot a Union soldier when she thought he insulted her mother. I felt sure that Eli knew that story as well as many others, and annoyed though I was to give up nearly an entire day to call on Mrs. Greenhow and to once again surrender to Eli's dark arts, I confess that I looked forward to meeting her in person, and perhaps having a glimpse of her extraordinary young daughter. I could not tell if I should feel disgusted by the thought of a young child virtually imprisoned with her mother, or inspired that mother and daughter chose to stay together, no matter what. *Really, Victoria,* I upbraided myself, *you are a fine one to make assumptions about how one should behave.*

As I mused, a carriage went by, and its front wheel splashed hard into a ditch. Eli pulled me out of harm's way as I watched the dark, ill-smelling mud splash nearby. He tucked my arm into his, and I felt a cruel moment of loss, that feeling of being watched over, cared for, truly treasured by someone. I had that once, and now, Eli's rote gallantry reminded me of what would never be mine.

"Sometimes," I said to Eli, "I think the two of us are destined to go our wicked ways together. Most mornings I wake up and do not know who is and who is not a traitor. I'm sure I must be."

"To be a traitor," said Eli, "you have to have a fixed side to be on. I do not, and you should not."

"You're right. Fixed sides are what got us into this predicament. I curse this war, I curse the blue and the gray.

We are wasting time and money, and worst of all, we are spilling blood."

Eli patted the top of my hand with a familiar touch. "Don't waste your time cursing, dear Vic. There is so much more to do, and we shall do it. When we get back from Mrs. Greenhow's, we will devise a new strategy."

I squeezed Eli's hand, but in all aspects I saw very little advantage of planning some new scheme. As it happened, I would come to know far more about Eli's scheme than anyone could wish. And despite my reservations, I, too, would find myself a serious student of the art of wartime deception. A spy? A turncoat? A traitor? These were all terms that suggested there was a side that was right and a side that was wrong, but that's the unquestioning way men see things. Who can blame them? Their commanders think only of progress: taking this hill, destroying this regiment, marching ever forward into filth and blood and death. And at the end, what?

We women are all Ariadne, looking for the thread that can guide us through the labyrinth and spin us home. As the train pulled into Richmond, I thought of that labyrinth and the mythological Minotaur who lurked there. It would take all I had not to make a misstep in that maze, and disappear forever.

CHAPTER 14

GABRIEL'S JOURNAL, 1862

> *"Once let the black man get upon his person the brass letter, U.S., let him get an eagle on his button, and a musket on his shoulder and bullets in his pocket, there is no power on earth that can deny that he has earned the right to citizenship."*
>
> — Frederick Douglass

I have two pleasures in life: women and my bugle. My employer, Mr. Allan Pinkerton, heard me pass this remark one day and asked, "And your work with us, keeping this great Union safe and secure, is that not a pleasure as well?"

"Do you want a fancy answer?" I asked. "Or do you want the truth?"

Mr. Pinkerton preferred a fancy answer, it seemed clear to me, and therefore I found something to commend. "Your employment has provided me with a unique experience, sir. And although going one thousand feet into the air initially filled my soul with fear, I will confess that my journeys in Professor Lowe's balloon are ones I shall never forget."

Pinkerton raised an eyebrow. I believe he could not

discern if I was making a jest or telling the truth. I was, in fact, speaking plain. Professor Thaddeus Lowe is a genius, I believe. His great care in designing balloons that would stand up to the rigors of military use was notable. The finest, sturdiest silk and cotton were used, and then swabbed all over with some magic elixir of varnish that Professor Lowe had invented. No problem was insoluble to Professor Lowe, appointed our Chief Aeronaut by the President of these United States, Abraham Lincoln. Last year, I first was recruited to visit the sky aboard the *Intrepid*. I do not have the skills of the brave aeronauts, but I have a skill nearly as crucial: I am a telegrapher, a man of speed with the key, a man who is ready to watch, record, and send information about the number, condition, and movement of Confederate troops.

On my first adventure, as I clambered into the small, swaying basket, I had two conflicting thoughts. First, that if I should survive, I would have a fine tale to tell Victoria. And the second was that I would be so paralyzed by fear that I would be unable to perform my duties as key operator.

Now that I have undertaken five journeys, the fear has abated, and it was the truth I spoke to Mr. Pinkerton. It is thrilling to be one thousand feet in the air. We are safe from the enemy if they spot us, because no shot can reach that high. And unlike some balloon craft, we are tethered, which gives at least the illusion of control. And although I have been sympathetic to Mr. Douglass's calls to serve in the Union army, I prefer the odds of survival serving in my current post. In fact, I am becoming a balloon enthusiast.

The Confederates were using balloon craft for surveillance as well, but they did not have Professor Lowe leading the way, and the Rebs had fewer craft and fewer successful reconnaissance adventures. The ingenious Lowe had even devised a way to inflate the balloons in the field. Working from his design and instructions, the Navy Yard built movable hydrogen-gas-generation wagons. And though Professor Lowe has a rival in the construction and use of his reconnaissance balloons in the very excitable Mr. John LaMountain, when I am putting my life in someone's hands, I prefer the more scientifically inclined professor.

However, I do question his judgment in incorporating a very large likeness of General McClellan's face on the *Intrepid*. If I was a Confederate soldier and saw that visage, floating God-like over the earth, I would be insulted and angry, and would think that my resolve to fight and my hatred of the Union troops would be increased many times over. I once hazarded that thought to Professor Lowe, and he narrowed his eyes at me. "You can say anything you like to me, Gabriel, but you must take care how you speak to others. No one likes being questioned in war. It is life or death, and we must choose boldly and decisively what we will do. The *Intrepid* is my finest gift to the Union, and I believe General McClellan is proud to know his likeness soars high above."

I wiped my face clean of expression and nodded in apparent agreement. "It is a marvel you have created, Professor. And I am deeply honored to be part of your team."

Once I would have attempted to further engage Professor Lowe in this conversation, debating back and forth on what risks are worth taking. But I have learned that even the friendliest of my battlefield comrades does not feel first loyalty to me, no matter what services I provide. I am a fine telegrapher, swift with the key and accurate in the transmission, and really, that is all there is to know. At moments like that, I miss Victoria more than ever. She loves a good argument and fiercely stands her ground, and expects me to stand my own as we do friendly battle. In my loneliest hours, when not even my horn provides consolation, I think of Victoria as my tether; not holding me fast to the ground, not trapped, but held with the silken threads of love. She would scoff at that image, but I do not care. I breathe deeply and imagine I can catch her very essence: fresh peach, a little lilac, and underneath it all, the heat generated by the flint-on-steel of her character. Sometimes I think of that heat and I must steady myself; just imagining the touch of Victoria when I am far away is enough to make me light-headed.

My horn and my women, I say, *those are my pleasures.* But the reality is this: There is only one woman now, Victoria. She is a ripe and blushing peach to me, and she is forbidden fruit.

CHAPTER 15

MAGGIE
OXFORD

Ole Miss won the party, but not the game. And so Phoebe was recovering from the disappointment with a little lie-down, while Michael was working his way slowly through the treasures of Square Books and I was back in the henhouse with Uncle Beau, asking questions about things I didn't understand. I had identified two puzzles already and I was only halfway through the museum. Beau had given me permission to take things off the wall to look more closely, so I had a little pile perched on a carved mahogany table, and I was ready to pepper him with questions.

"Fire away, honey," he said.

I picked up an elaborately framed photograph of a pensive woman dressed all in black, her arm encircling the waist of a little girl who looked almost as determined as the woman. "Who are they? And why are they both dressed so elegantly when it looks as if the woman is sitting in an abandoned courtyard?" Her ruched skirts billowed directly into dirt and stones.

"That is the infamous Rose Greenhow, the queen of the Confederate spies," said Beau. "And that is Little Rose, her daughter."

"And where are they?"

"They are in the Old Capitol Prison in Washington, DC."

"Wait, what? Her daughter went to prison with her?"

"Yes, indeed. And Little Rose was, if I understand correctly, almost as strong-minded as her mother."

"And why do you have this photograph?"

"It was in one of your grandmother Alma's hatboxes. And you're wondering why she had it?"

"Exactly. I keep thinking about clearing out Alma and Morris's house after she died and Papa Morris went to the assisted living place near us. She had file cabinets of thank-you notes and recipes and dress patterns and tons and tons of photographs of our family, but I don't remember seeing anything like this." Something flitted across my mind and I struggled to grasp it.

"Except..." I said and stopped. "Except for that steamer trunk in the laundry room; it had a bunch of old photos and documents from her days as a nurse in World War II."

"That's fifty-five years after Rose Greenhow's time," said Beau.

"I know, but I just have a feeling I need to go back and look at that stuff. I just wish Papa Morris's memory hadn't gone missing."

"We can't do anything about that, honey."

I put the framed photo back on the little table so that Rose and Little Rose stared out at us.

"So what did Rose Greenhow have to do with our family?"

"We don't exactly know. It's mostly family lore and fanciful stories," said Beau. "But Rose was very famous, hobnobbed with Dolley Madison and John C. Calhoun, and was very instrumental in some early Confederate victories. The Battle at Bull Run, for example. Rose's network of contacts let her know that the Union was gathering forces at Manassas. She got the news to Beauregard, so the Rebs were prepared and took the day."

"I think I must have a very outdated picture of what women spies look like — I keep picturing Mata Hari and Josephine Baker. Rose Greenhow looks like an ordinary, but well-off, lady of leisure."

"Ah, this is where knowing a little more about history is quite useful. The Civil War was an historic moment for women spies — Belle Boyd, Rose Greenhow, Harriet Tubman, they're the famous names, but there were hundreds of women spies on both sides, Confederate and Union."

"I had no idea," I said. "You called her *Mrs.* Greenhow, right?"

"Yes, she was married to a distinguished man, Dr. Robert Greenhow. She was a beauty, and he was a catch — he had degrees in medicine and law and had worked for President Buchanan. Marrying Dr. Greenhow was a stroke of brilliance for Rose. She was already known for her beauty and her charms, and becoming the wife of a prominent man immediately catapulted her into Washington's high society." Beau placed the photo back on the table. "Rose should have run for public office — she had great people instincts, and according to what I've read, really could charm the birds right out of the trees. But she was born about 150 years too early."

"I should say so. Women didn't even have the right

to vote in Rose's day. Did her husband approve of her spying career?"

"Ah, well, that's still another story. Dr. Greenhow died after a fall in San Francisco, while Rose was away visiting their older children. They had been married almost twenty years, but Rose was a fairly young widow, and still very beautiful, and she was a Southerner through and through. So, after a few years as a merry widow, she was looking for something more substantive to do. That 'something' was an offer she couldn't refuse: to discover and share information about the battle plans of the Union armies in various theaters of war. She became the link to critical information — everything from troop movements to who was recruitable, so she could broaden her network. Eventually she had dozens of spies and countless informants — witting and unwitting — in her control."

"This is way better than anything I ever learned about the Civil War," I said.

"I always thought you might be the one who got interested in all this," said Beau. "Since your grandmother Alma had a career as a wartime nurse, not to mention Victoria herself."

Phoebe stuck her head in the door. "I am restored, and we shall live to fight another day. Come have some iced tea or a lovely cocktail, you two, and Beau, don't be talking that poor girl's ears off."

"I'm the one who's being a pest, Phoebe," I protested. "I think we're just getting to the good stuff. I need to know what happened to Rose and to Little Rose, and just how she pried that info out of people."

"Oh, the ways of women are complex and nefarious," said Beau. "More after dinner."

"Phoebe, we'll be right there," I said. "Can I just ask Beau about one piece of paper?"

"Be quick," she said. "Michael's back, and I know he's ready for an adult beverage."

I picked up a document in a plastic sleeve. It was the color of jasmine tea, and the creases in the sheet made it hard to read. "This is about Victoria, isn't it?" I asked. "I see her name there, but I don't quite know what it means — she was remanded to Old Capitol Prison herself, is that right? Why?"

Beau sighed. "I wish I knew exactly, but from the document, if you look at it with a loupe, you'll get some idea."

He pulled a loupe out of his pocket and handed it over. "Put it right down on the paper and look. See, right there?"

"Victoria Alma Cardworthy," I read, "is remanded to Old Capitol Prison for...espionage and..." I looked up. "Bigamy? Does that say bigamy?"

CHAPTER 16

LETTER FROM VICTORIA TO GABRIEL, 1862

"I had been away long enough to become demoralized. It had been snowing for some days, and the snow was melting, which made every thing damp and comfortless. A hospital is the most cheerless place in the world, and the last place I would remain in from choice. If it were not for the sake of the wounded and sick men, I do not think I could possibly stand it."

— Kate Cumming, from
Kate: The Journal of a Confederate Nurse

My dearest G,

I wake thinking of you, I fall asleep thinking of you: your dear face, your kind hands, the place between shoulder and chest where I feel as if I have come home. You know, we women of tall stature do not find that place to nestle so readily. Perhaps my feelings for you are just an accident of height!

You have asked me to tell you a simple story about how I spend a day at Chimborazo Hospital, and I shall comply.

But you must know, first off, that one never spends just a day. It is often a day and then an evening, and then we welcome the dawn and must sometimes start all over again.

There are relatively few women in service at Chimborazo: some nurses and matrons and a few like me, roaming spirits who go where they are most needed. I will mention more about that later, because it is part of the news I have to share. Most of the nurses at Chimborazo are still men, many of whom had been wounded and are near recovery now, some simply assigned to the tasks that need most attention. And then we have a group of slaves who have been loaned-on-hire to the hospital by their masters. In some ways, of course, the slaves are best fitted to this work. Many had worked in households, taking care of master, mistress, and children, so they know how to create comfort where there is pain, how to cook and sew and clean, how to wrest some organization out of chaos.

Of course, the chaos here at Chimborazo is relatively minor. Most of the injured who come to us have been moved from the battlefield hospitals, and frankly, it is only the strongest who survive that transport.

It is such an odd word, "Chimborazo," is it not? I have learned of its origins and you, who always have a dozen whys to pose in any conversation, will be interested, I feel sure. The hospital is named for Chimborazo Hill, which lays at the eastern edge of the fine city of Richmond. And it is not a word that falls easily from anyone's tongue in the beginning. That is likely because it is named for Mount

Chimborazo, which is a volcano in Ecuador! This world is already far too explosive for my taste these days. Wherever I go, either I hear the terrible sound of cannons and muskets or I imagine I do, so I am not enjoying even the idea of our hospital as a place waiting to erupt.

But I have gone far afield from answering your request, and so I will try again. We begin most days the same way, with the most important medicines in hand: soap, water, and decent food. Somehow, no matter how much pain a man is in, it is restorative to do nothing more than wash his hands and face and then, even though it can be so painful and tender, to wash his wounds as well. Then we deliver breakfast: some bread or biscuit, with butter if we are fortunate enough to find some, meat for strength, and for those in the most fragile state, an egg, just coddled. Oh, that is sometimes the most wrenching part of our duties, though. More than once I have delivered breakfast to a young soldier, and returned to collect his dish and found that while I was about my work, he had drawn his last breath.

I do not shrink from the hardest work of nursing, cleaning up after the endless surgeries for amputation, cleaning up when the dread dysentery strikes. However, the sight of a young man who had been, just minutes before looking at a simple coddled egg and biscuit and thinking about gaining strength, and suddenly the world shifts for him. Each time that happens I feel that we have failed, and I feel a renewed sense of rage at war itself. The globe keeps spinning as the scientists tell us, but one beautiful life, still fresh-in-the-making, has simply slipped off the planet. I do not understand the rhyme or reason of this. And then it is often my duty to assist in writing letters home to a family about this death. There is no sadder, more heartbreaking work. But I take a deep breath and remember that my grief is nothing compared to that of the family that has lost a son or brother, and that it will not provide one iota of comfort to see bitter words on the page.

The rest of my day is often a blur. I meet with the matron, who is chief of the nurses, and I supervise the linens, making sure we have enough, that they are clean and mended. I bring morphine to those most in pain, and at the end of the day, after supper, I sit with those who are too weak to ask for help. "What do you need?" I ask each wounded or ill soldier, sitting at the bedside and leaning close so I can be heard. One young man, an apprentice blacksmith from Mobile, gave me the best answer I ever heard. "I don't need anything," he said, "but a kind word." I remembered that, long after he left the hospital and returned to his regiment.

And those are my days, dear G, probably not as dangerous or exciting as yours, but in a way we are both at work taking care of our fellow human beings. Oh, one other note of interest. I have struck up an acquaintanceship with a quite remarkable doctor from Richmond, Dr. James B. McCaw. He is young to be so accomplished, and he is very, very much the head of Chimborazo, ambitious to run the best hospital possible. He has, in fact, organized

all these wooden buildings we occupy as a small city. He
is a demon for planning and is relentless in his pursuit of
resources to take care of our patients. For whatever reason, we have come to like and respect each other, and he
occasionally honors me by asking my opinion about some
matter, perhaps about food or about restoring the use of an
injured limb. He knows I have cared for Union soldiers as
well, and I believe he suspects I may have acquired useful
information about medical matters from the "other side."

Dr. McCaw is also eager to supplement what foodstuffs
the Confederacy provides, and so he is very happy when I
take a few hours to ride Courage outside of town and go on
a foraging expedition. I settle canvas bags on either side of
my horse so that I can bring back something, anything that
is fresh. Sometimes I find windfall apples, bruised but perfect for making an apple pudding, or I find wild nettles, and
can trim them down to their tender hearts to boil gently
for a fresh vegetable. I look also for herbs that have healing
properties, chamomile to soothe a sleepless night, yarrow
to heal cuts, feverfew for headaches. You would laugh, G,
to see me ride in with all kinds of greens and wispy blooms
bulging out of my saddlebags, and generally out of my
sleeves and hair as well; one must duck under trees and slip
between hedges to be a successful forager. I am sure I look
like the Madwoman of the Garden Gate when I return. Oh,
I must be very tired and addled this evening! How could I
have forgotten that you, of all people, know precisely how
I look when I have been on a foraging adventure? How

could I lose track of our first meeting?

Although I still forage with a serious purpose, hoping to find treasures to bring back to the kitchen, I must confess that I also ride because it restores me to be away from all the grief and suffering at Chimborazo. Courage asks nothing of me but oats and exercise. We are silent together, which is also welcome, and we work as a team, anticipating each other's next move. I try to return to Chimborazo by dark, but a few evenings ago, I had to wait out a thunderstorm before I headed back. By then the twilight had faded, and the sky was as dark as that beautiful blue velvet dress your sister stitched for me. The stars were out, unaffected by the sorrow and blood of the war, just twinkling away on all of us, those who wear blue and those who wear gray. It was so beautiful, I couldn't help but think of that fateful December day in 1860 when South Carolina seceded from the Union and became an independent entity. Charlestonians celebrated as if it was a party instead of a war being announced. There were fireworks overhead, church bells rang, and cannons sundered the air. Do you remember how fast it all happened after that? In six short weeks, South Carolina was joined in revolt by Mississippi, Florida, Alabama, Louisiana, and Texas, and by June, the count was eleven. Thinking about those early days, days of fireworks and parties and balls honoring the Confederate States of America, makes me dizzy with nausea. What earthly reason did anyone have to celebrate?

Dear G, I have strayed far from your request, and I

know that your feelings about this distressing war run even deeper than mine. Here is the only thing I can say. It was blood that brought us together, and that blood was occasioned by war. I care nothing for those fireworks in the sky; they are inconsequential to the fireworks you have stirred in my heart and in my soul. Some day we will say and do everything that matters.

Until then, until we are together,

Your Victoria

CHAPTER 17

LETTER FROM GABRIEL TO VICTORIA, 1862

Beloved Vic,

You have pleased me no end with your story about a day and more at Chimborazo. I felt as if I were in those rooms with you, being your shadow as you sat at those bedsides. If ever I find myself in mortal danger of losing my life, I, too, would want you at my side. Truth to tell, going up in the balloons for Mr. Pinkerton often makes me feel as if I am in mortal danger. But now, because I have grown somewhat accustomed to these excursions, and I concentrate so deeply on my telegraph duties, the fear loses its bite. Of course I would not want to put you in any danger, but I often think about how much enjoyment there would be if the two of us could share an adventure in the air. I know you, and it would not even occur to you to be afraid!

This evening, I am inspired to write to you about words. Because you are such a well-spoken woman, you often set me to considering the world of language. I am conscious sometimes that your fine talk can cut fools and pretenders to the quick, and I do have some fear about you making enemies. But here I am, wandering off the subject. Of late, when I walk out at night, I think of how meaning-less some words can be. You and I, for example, would be branded as criminals, as perhaps we should be. I am a thief and a smuggler; you are a spy.

What have I stolen, you ask? I have stolen something more precious than gold or gems. I have stolen the lan-guage of an educated man right out from under my former employer's nose. And would he mind? I do not know. When I was a boy, he seemed to take pleasure in the fact that I learned to read so easily and eagerly, that I could converse with guests, and that women found me of interest. I'm sure that was simply because I was a two-footed variation on the dogs and horses he put out to stud. "Productivity in the fields, and productivity in the bed," he used to say.

And smuggling, well, those days seem to be fading, but oh, they were filled with all the emotions known to man: apprehension, excitement, and, when we were successful, a feeling of triumph I cannot explain. Danger must be a love potion, dear Vic, because in the height of my smuggling days, when we had heard from across the River Jordan that another family had reached the north country safely, had stepped onto Canadian soil, I would think of you and long to feel the power of your body, top to toe, against mine. Whenever I hold you, I am grateful right down to my bones for this tall, strong, red-headed woman who is a match for any man. Certainly for this poor smuggler.

Of course, like you, I also have another identity. I am

a Pinkerton man, and my comrades on the field and in the air seem grateful for my contributions in transmitting information. I suppose, in some way, that makes you and me comrades as well. While I am not as skilled in the art of espionage as you are, we both trade in information.

But you, Victoria, have a public identity as a nurse, which makes you exalted over all other women, at least in my opinion. You are a true angel of the battlefield, like Miss Nightingale, and well before Miss Dorothea Dix was elevated to her position as chief of nurses, well before she rightly insisted that nurses were to give equal care to boys in blue and boys in gray, you were quietly living that practice. I admire you for that. It is good that I let you know what I admire about your conscience, lest you think that all my admiration is frittered away on your face and form.

So here we are, a spy and a smuggler, a nurse and a telegraph operator who conquered his fears of height. To me, we are a fine pair. To the wider world, well, that is another matter.

CHAPTER 18

MAGGIE
OXFORD

"Phoebe," I said once we were settled on the back patio, drinks in hand and pre-dinner snacks nearby, "you are one avant-garde cook. I love this cold black-eyed pea relish — I've never had anything like it."

"It's Mississippi Caviar," she said. "Isn't it yummy? The Lamar Lounge makes some version of it, but I like mine better because I stuff it in those little Middle Eastern bread pockets, you know, pita bread? It's a...a...what do you young people call it? A 'mash-up,' that's it, and it keeps those black-eyed peas un-mushy."

"Beau," said Michael, "is it too late? I'd really like to rethink the whole one-true-love thing and ask for your wife's hand in marriage. Ironed sheets, un-mushy black-eyed peas — does it get better than that?"

Phoebe and I sighed in unison. "So," I said, "now that we're fortified with adult beverages, Uncle Beau, can you explain the whole bigamy thing on that arrest record or whatever it was? Was my great-great-great-grandmother truly a spy and a bigamist? Can that be right?"

"You know these old documents, honey," said Beau. "We don't know how accurate or authentic any of them might be."

"Why wouldn't they be?"

"Lots of reasons. Before, during, and after the War Between the States there was a lot of prevaricating and document adjustment. Deserters who obtained forged documents of discharge, men who claimed to have been wounded when they'd simply shot themselves in the foot to escape service. Plantation owners who claimed that black freemen were runaway slaves, and so they essentially imprisoned them. And there were terribly brave and noble people as well who were living lies — women who dressed as men to go to war with their husbands, or simply to get a taste of independence. It was, as the man says in *A Tale of Two Cities*, 'the best of times, it was the worst of times.' And to make getting information even more of a challenge, Southerners don't like speaking directly, as I would think you know by now."

"Oh, yes," I said. "Prying information out of the cousins is like going into an archaeological dig with a set of measuring spoons — and you can only use the one-eighth teaspoon."

"You can always ask us," said Phoebe, helpfully. She held up the bottle of Buffalo bourbon and raised her eyebrows at Michael. "More, honey?"

He shook his head. "Phoebe, you're trying to get me tipsy."

"No, I'm not. And," she added firmly, "I am not like the rest of this 'silence-is-golden' family. I am happy to spill the goods, if I know anything. That," she said with a cat-eating-the-canary smile, "is the privilege of being an in-law."

"I can trust your discretion, my dear," said Beau.

"Oh no you can't," crowed Phoebe. "All these secrets, secrets, secrets in your hoity-toity family."

"Oh, goody," I said. "I love secrets."

"Now wait just a minute," protested Beau. "We do have some family honor to uphold, but I don't believe in prevaricating. How could I be a genealogist without wanting to know the truth?"

Phoebe cocked one eyebrow and gave Beau one of those knowing Southern-wife smiles. "Well, that's so true, darlin'. But I say it's time for dinner, don't you think?"

After dinner, Phoebe and Michael dove back into their books, and Beau and I were drawn right back to the henhouse.

"Please, sir," I said to Beau. "May I have some more? I want to understand how Victoria ended up in prison. From what little I know, she sounded heroic — taking care of soldiers, Union and Confederate. What reason on earth would someone have to put her in prison?"

"Honey, that's what's so intriguing about history. We can't know for sure, despite all our best efforts — time has passed, and all the players who could tell us some version of the truth are dead and buried. And your great-great-great-grandmother lived in a time of tumult and war. The truth is not always convenient."

I scrutinized Beau's kind face. "You're not telling me something."

"It's not that. I just think you'll understand more if you do some discovery yourself."

"Okay, I'm in. Where do I start?"

"Start with the letters. Alma knew Victoria. I think

they must have been very close, and Alma was Victoria's most faithful correspondent. And you'll also find a little journal that Victoria kept. There weren't many entries in there, but enough to...well, you'll see."

"Letters?" I asked. "There were letters? And a journal too?"

Beau nodded. "In the little wooden cabinet that's locked up in your bedroom closet." He pulled his key ring out of his pocket and painstakingly eased an age-darkened key off the ring.

"How come I've never seen any of that material before?" I asked. "You're always sending genealogical news out in your quarterly summary about the Cardworthys. How come...."

He handed me the key. "Just don't stay up all night."

CHAPTER 19

ALMA, 1941

Dearest Granny Vic,

Thank you, thank you, thank you.

Thank you for standing up for me with Mama and Grandma Hester. I know they are very upset about my news. At first that made me angry, that they thought I would not be smart enough or brave enough to serve my country. But as I cooled down, remembering that a nurse must stay calm and reasonable no matter what, I began to see that they are simply worried.

Daddy won't even speak to me, except to try to bully me out of my decision. He keeps asking where I learned to be so cruel, how I could worry my mother so much by going off to war. But I have come to realize that if I want to be considered an independent, adult woman, I must behave like one! You gave me very good advice. You said, "Do not argue. Simply state your case and tell your parents how much you love them and that you hope to make them proud."

And so that is what I am doing. Thank you also for sending me off on this adventure with your beautiful necklace. Knowing that it was a gift from someone you love makes it very precious. I love the fine silver setting and the beautiful aquamarine, and the fact that it is the birthstone that we share. Most of all I love that you have worn this necklace for so long and now you are entrusting it to me. I will not let you down, Granny Vic, and I will take good care of your necklace. Although as I write this, I hear you saying to me, "The necklace is meant to take good care of you, my Alma."

But now I must say the most important thank you of all. I am so grateful that you have talked to me about love. This is not a topic we discuss in my house, even though I know my parents love each other very much. When I thought my heart was broken last spring, when that stuck-up prig Teddy Prayhorn told me that he "had to" marry someone from his dim-witted mama's country-club circle, you did not sympathize. Instead, you said, "He is not worthy to empty your slop jar," and I started laughing so hard, even as I kept protesting, "Granny, no one has a slop jar anymore. We have toilets!"

"I disagree," you said. "That young man is a slop jar."

And then you made me tea and poured a little something "medicinal" in there. So, I did feel better, but a part of me — and I am ashamed to admit this — thought how on earth could you know anything about love? And Granny, it isn't because you are older, it is because you have always seemed so independent to me. I never knew your husband, my great-grandfather Jules, because he died before I was born. And so I have never seen you with a man you love, romantically, I mean.

But the story you told me today, on our birthdays, shocked and thrilled me. You have loved three men! Great-grandfather Jules and two others. I felt as if you were Scheherazade telling me stories about an enchanted castle, filled with hidden rooms and handsome suitors in each one, all vying for the hand of my beautiful Great-Granny Vic.

Yes, I am being silly, but truly, Granny Vic, the stories sounded like something out of the moving pictures. It was so hard to leave you after our conversation, but I know you were very tired. I am so honored that you talked so frankly with me.

Tomorrow I must go shopping in the morning to finish off the list the US Army Corps has provided me. I will show you the list; I think it must be very different from what you packed when you rode off on Courage so many years ago. But I would love to continue our conversation, so unless you are too worn out, I will stop by after lunch. Neilson's has a new addition to their candy counter, I hear, and guess what? I think that very strong peppermint is involved. If that is so, I will arrive with a little red-striped bag for you.

With much love and admiration, and in anticipation of more revelations to come,

Alma

CHAPTER 20

VICTORIA'S JOURNAL, 1862

If war has taught me one terrible lesson already, it is this: Everything changes in one moment. A battle lost. A life lost. A beloved family home burned to the ground. But what I did not understand was that life can change in a moment for the better as well. Instead of sorrow over another loss, another heartbreak, in fact, we human beings can feel transformed by joy. And that joy can enter our lives in such an unexpected time or place.

Today, I experienced exactly that transformation, and I must commit it to paper before I forget one moment of what transpired.

Courage and I were out on an early spring forage again. Fresh vegetables had been particularly hard to come by, so after morning rounds, I saddled up and rode out to the wild fields a few miles from the hospital. I looped the reins over a low branch on a live oak and fed Courage a handful of oats, although I know he longed for an apple or carrot. "I share that longing," I said to him, "but we eat what's in front of us, my friend." I hitched up my skirts and picked my way through the soft, green grass looking for edibles. I had to stop and look up for a moment. Though the world was at war, the ground on which I stood, right then and there, was downright Eden-like. The fresh smell of spring, the damp loam, the tiny crocuses of yellow and deep purple, and not one soul in sight. I felt dizzy with the desire to lie down on that soft green and close my eyes. "Enough!" I said aloud, and continued, my eyes downcast, scanning for nourishment. My pace quickened when I saw what looked like wild mustard just through a copse of young trees. I am a careful forager; after all, one does not wish to bestow healthful greenery on our patients only to see them fall deathly ill from some misidentified wild plant. But mustard! Ah, it is unmistakable. It is tangy, it is nutritious, and it is green! I spread a large piece of muslin on the ground, knelt, and happily began cutting the tangy emerald-and-ruby-colored greens with the hunting knife my brother gave me on my twelfth birthday. The ground was damp, and my skirt was growing soggy and soiled, but I was so delighted to find the mustard greens that I found myself softly singing my favorite minstrel song:

> "Nellie Bly has a voice like the turtle dove,
> I hear it in the meadow, and I hear it in the grove;
> Nellie Bly has a heart warm as a cup of tea,
> And bigger than the sweet potato down in Tennessee."

I sat back on my heels and began tying the four corners of the muslin together to secure the greens for the ride back home. And then I heard Courage whinny, as if someone was near, and then the next chorus of "Nellie Bly" came through the trees. A sweet, pure tenor voice sang, "Heigh Nellie, Nellie Ho, Listen, love to me, I'll sing for you and play for you a dulcet melody."

I walked under the oak boughs into the greensward, where I'd left Courage tied. First, I saw the tail end of a carrot disappear into his mouth. And then I saw his gentle benefactor, you, stroking his neck and watching me.

Mr. Edgar Allen Poe came to my mind, and his story, "The Tell-Tale Heart." I was not frightened at all, although one might expect an unescorted young woman meeting a man alone in the woods to be frightened. But it was not fear that caused my telltale heart to hammer in my chest, it was not fear that took my breath away.

It was you. We looked at each other, and I felt as if those mustard greens I had held so close to my heart were some essential drug, some intoxicant that I had breathed and thereby conjured you right in front of me.

With one hand still on Courage's neck, you lifted your battered hat to me. And then you sang the chorus of "Nelly Bly" one more time.

You stepped away from Courage, and I said, "You, sir, have a beautiful voice."

You inclined your head in a bow. Then you said, "And you, madam, have a beautiful face."

I have no idea what possessed me, but I could not help myself. I whispered, "Oh, no, sir, you have the most beautiful face of all." I walked a few steps to you, and I held out my hand. We shook like comrades, my white hand in your black hand. And my heart on display, for anyone to see.

Thus did we begin.

CHAPTER 21

VICTORIA'S JOURNAL, 1941

What have I done? That was my first thought upon awakening this morning. Why have I opened the first chapter of this messy, complicated book I call my life? And to Alma, my darling, my beloved great-granddaughter? I am a fool. When she knows, if she knows…then I could be ruined.

And then I nearly laughed aloud at my vanity. How can I be "ruined"? I am an old woman just a few steps from the grave. Who will care about my past? And if I tell Alma, she will keep my secret. Or she will not. She is strong-minded, my Alma. She will, perhaps, find my past interesting, even amusing. When I tell, if I tell…I know her. She will make her own decision.

As it happened, Alma preempted me. "Granny Vic," she called from outside my door just before 10 a.m. "Can you let me in? My hands are full!"

I opened the door and there she was, dressed in her Sunday best, a beautiful navy suit trimmed all around with white piping. Her pocketbook was tucked under her arm, and her arms were full of flowers. "These are lovely," I said. "But extravagant! You shouldn't be spending your money on flowers for me."

"Sorry, Granny Vic. They're not for you. I want to go to the cemetery with you this morning and put flowers on the graves of the gentlemen you loved before Great-Grandpa Jules."

I started to protest. And then I realized what a gift Alma was giving me. She would learn my secret at the cemetery without me having to speak a word.

I do not know if this is happenstance or not, but I live very close to the Episcopalian cemetery, and so Alma and I set out on the path from my home, just slightly up the hill. "Now, Granny Vic," she said, "I am putting you on notice. You may not make that old joke again about what a swift journey you will have to heaven when you die because you live so conveniently close."

I stopped and caught my breath. "I don't have to make that joke today. You have now officially made it for me."

She laughed and shook her finger at me. "You outwit me every time," she said, as the two tallest, fanciest memorials came into view.

I know I slow Alma down a very great deal, but I love to take her arm and listen to her chatter away about all the happenings in town, and who wore what to the early service at College Hill Presbyterian Church, the oldest house of worship in Lafayette County. At the entrance, I stopped again to catch my breath. I had not been here for some time, and I closed my eyes to envision my two destinations. They came to me as clear as day, and with a firmer step

I set off without Alma's assistance. I walked past the two banker showoffs, with their tall monuments within inches of each other in matching heights: J.W.T. Falkner and Bem Price. I stop a moment, and Alma and I exchange glances. "Men," she says. "Is it indelicate to say that they will compete about size always and forever?"

But I had the bit in my teeth, and so I walked another fifty yards. We stopped, and I gestured at the grave in front of us with my walking stick, and Alma knelt to brush away the debris on the stone. She read aloud: "Eli Mays, 1835–1892: You Made Me Laugh." She placed her bouquet of sweet peas, trailing jasmine, and zinnias on the gravesite.

Then she stood and put her arm around me. "You were married to Mr. Mays?" I nodded. "And did you love him very much? I would think you would love a man who made you laugh."

"I grew to love him," I said. "He was in love with me for a long time, since we were children, I think, and we… worked together during the War Between the States. So it was not a great passion on my part, but he sacrificed much for me. And I was grateful." I felt the sun warming my back.

I could feel Alma's puzzlement. This is not the story she expected to hear. "Granny Vic," she said tentatively. "Can you tell me about Mr. Mays's sacrifice?"

I began to tremble.

"You're shaking. Come sit down." She guided me to a stone bench, and we sat there a while. Suddenly the air was boisterous with music. Three hermit thrush had found the teetery old birdbath in the middle of the cemetery. They splashed and sang and danced around like drunken fools. I took a deep breath.

"I will tell you about Eli soon, but now, I want to introduce you to my other husband, my..." I struggled to say the words. "My sweetheart." Alma looked at once puzzled and worried. I could tell she thought poor Granny Vic was finally going around the bend and not coming back. I patted her hand. "Don't fret, child. You don't need to worry about me. I'm fine. You'll see. Just give an old lady a hand up." Alma helped me to my feet, and we began the walk across the grass scattered with grand monuments and weeping stone angels. At the edge of the cemetery we passed the small sign that read: St. Peter's, Colored Cemetery. And we walked in together.

CHAPTER 22

MAGGIE
OXFORD

"Victoria," I whispered. "I want to know you." I placed the letter on top of the small pile of those I'd already read; I closed the journal and placed the palm of my hand on top of the soft oxblood cover. It felt warm to the touch, as if Victoria herself had just finished writing and put it aside.

I rubbed my eyes furiously. The strain of making out Victoria's shaky hand and Alma's fine handwriting was exhausting. But how could I stop? Who was this brave woman? And who was she spying for? And why was all this a secret? At that, I laughed aloud. A spy? What white woman fell in love with a black man during the Civil War? Yes, I could see the need for being secretive.

The door between the bedroom and Beau's museum space creaked open. Michael, in navy boxers with Hotty Toddy stenciled in cardinal on one leg, leaned against the door frame. "Maggie? It's two in the morning. Come to bed."

I opened my mouth to say I couldn't, and to start rattling off what I'd read and the dozens of questions I had. But there he was, illuminated by the moonlight streaming in from the window, and I thought, *Victoria needs to know that I believe in love as well. To be worthy of her.*

I gestured to his boxers. "Nice undergarments, Mr. Fiori."

He looked down. "They are, aren't they? A gift from Beau."

I stood up. "Two questions. Were they purchased at Neilson's? And are they...removable?"

The answer to each question was yes, as it turned out, and in honor of Victoria, we paid our own tribute to love. Hotty toddy indeed.

The next morning, I was up early and ready to start interrogating Beau. I found him outside in the garden, tying up his tomato-plant extravaganza branches so that they wouldn't touch the ground, so weighted down were they with late-fall heirlooms.

"Hey, honey," he called. "Come give me a hand for a minute with these love-apples." I picked up the green twine from the patio table and carried it over to the tomato patch. Together we staked and tied the branches.

Beau shook his head. "Well, it's not a work of art like Phoebe would have done, but she'll be pleased to see our rescue maneuvers. She's been fussing and worrying about even one of those not-yet-ripe babies falling to the ground. Somehow we just didn't get the tomato cages placed early enough this year."

We brushed off our hands and gathered the leftover stakes. "You didn't even blink when I called those tomatoes love-apples," said Beau as we walked to the house. The screen door squeaked, but when we walked into the kitchen, it still had the heavy quiet of people sleeping.

"Hey," I whispered. "I'm the granddaughter of Mississippi farmers. I've got to have some horticultural cred. I know that love-apples are one of the original names of tomatoes. And I know they're a fruit, not a vegetable."

We washed our hands at the big double sink. He let out a low snort. "Michael's right. You are a little miss know-it-all."

"Oh," I said, "I've got more dope on love-apples. No one's up — let's take a walk to the square and score some coffee."

We strolled past comfortable houses, including the Neilson family home, which was more mansion than house, and admired the gardens. Continuity matters in Mississippi, so everyone in town is proud to tell visitors that descendants of the Neilson family still own and run Oxford's only department store, founded in 1839 and still helping young women look their best for the historic version of sorority rush devised by Ole Miss.

As we walked, I delivered a short but, all modesty aside, useful mini-lecture on the love-apples. "The related Hebrew word is *dudaim*. Which means love-plants. And, of course, they are related to the sexy and dangerous *Mandragora officinalis,* and I believe a kissing cousin to the nightshades. Oh, and you know what else? Mandrake was the common name, and the story went that if you pulled the plant up by its roots — which looked weirdly like the shape of a human being, with two carrot-shaped dangling legs — you'd be condemned to hell."

"Makes gardening a mite dangerous."

I was on a roll. "Of course, there's always got to be

a French contingent if we're discussing the dangerous art of love, and in fact to the French, apples were
pommes d'amour, the apples of love. But then it was
the Spanish who eventually introduced tomatoes to the
rest of Europe, and as is their wont, of course, the Euro-
peans didn't quite trust the Spanish. And that, mixed up
with the deadly nightshade connection, is why people
thought they might be poisonous. I think it was an act
of daring to eat a love-apple. You know, risking everything for love."

Next to me, Beau had stopped and was leaning on a
pillar. I put my arm on his shoulder. "Beau? You okay?"

He was shaking, but he managed to nod. I stepped
back a moment and realized he was shaking with laughter. He patted my cheek. "Maggie, you get on a tear and
there is just no stopping you, is there?"

I sniffed. "Humph. I thought you were interested in
the mandrake."

"Honey, I can get interested in whatever wild tale
you're spinning. I'm just observing that once you've
got that engine revved up, there are no brakes on that
operation."

"I suppose you're not interested in more supersti-
tions about the love-apples."

"Are there more?" he asked faintly.

"It's okay. Let's just walk."

We'd come to the square, and we began a stroll
around its historic sides. A few coffee places just off the
square were open, and the fragrance of coffee drifted
out the windows. A few early-bird, up-and-at-'em tour-
ists were already climbing the stairs to the courthouse,
peering in the windows, stepping back to look at the cu-

pola on top, and then peering in again, hoping someone would open up. We stopped in front of Neilson's, and in a window I spotted many variations of Michael's boxers clothespinned to an artfully swinging clothesline.

"I've had a viewing of those boxers you bought Michael," I said. "I don't usually see him in boxers."

"That may be too much information for me, honey. But now that you've seen them, are you a convert?"

I smiled. "I try to be flexible in my opinion about whatever option he chooses."

Beau laughed. "Not your Auntie Phoebe. She forbade me to wear anything but boxers after we were married. She had some theory or other about keeping the air flowing around what she called 'the gentleman's parts.' "

We turned a corner and saw one of Oxford's holiest grails, the statue of William Faulkner, relaxing on a bench. Without speaking, we detoured just a few steps and settled ourselves next to him on the bench.

"I can see your Grandmother Alma sitting right here," he said. "She told me that it was a place that felt like home because she and her great-grandmother, Victoria, used to rest here when they were out for a walk."

Beau paused and looked away. I put my hand on his. "What's wrong, Beau?"

He swiped at his eyes. "Nothing, honey. I think about all that life — every new grandchild just wipes me out with love, and I think about how I may not see this one get married or that one become a parent."

"Why? What's wrong? Are you...ill, Beau?"

He laughed. "Not yet, no more than the usual aches and pains and a small stack of annoying pills my doctor makes me take. But I'm old, honey, and here's how that works — apparently it is not in God's plan for us to grow younger. And so it makes me hungry to hold my family even closer." He shook his head. "Of course that means different things to different people, but I cannot abide the thought that a grandchild or niece or nephew of mine will be left behind when I'm gone without mastering the rudiments of fishing. I don't have lots to offer, but I know my way around a line and a pole."

I linked my arm in his, and we watched as the square began to fill with life. Shopkeepers raised blinds and straightened welcome mats. Runners and walkers powered by. Evolved Southern dads pushed strollers on their mission — to let mom sleep in and bring her back a perfectly prepared single nonfat latte. Sleepy Ole Miss girls, decked out in sweats instead of picture-perfect dresses and full-on makeup, crept into the square for caffeine (coffee *or* Coke) and dished over Saturday night.

A gaggle of three walked by, deconstructing rush and condemning some poor Connecticut boy to isolation. "He didn't buy her flowers, and he showed up at the Grove in shorts and a T-shirt. You know...."

They all giggled. "That dog won't hunt," crowed another one.

After their little morning-after parade went by, I sighed. Beau said, "Now, not a one of those young ladies can hold a patch to you, Maggie."

I smiled. "Beau, you are so full of walkabout-on-air pudding."

"Your mama used to say that."

"Thinking about what lasts when we're gone...that's why you're letting me into Victoria's past, isn't it?"

CHAPTER 23

ALMA, 1941

Dearest Granny Vic,

I can hardly write you without weeping. And then I am ashamed of myself, because I am weeping over something that happened to you — and it is not my right to feel as strongly as I feel. I cannot even begin to imagine the terror you must have felt about being discovered, but still you went on, loving Mr. Gabriel, being...well, I guess you would say, a double agent? And through it all, caring for the wounded, whether they wore blue or gray or polka dots! You were a hero, Granny Vic, and I have never known a real live hero who didn't just exist in a book. There should be a book about you!

Now I am wandering around the mulberry bush when I want to say a few important things to you. I wrote myself a list last night so I wouldn't forget anything that I wanted to say. Here is my list:

1. Thank you for allowing me to visit Mr. Eli and Mr. Gabriel with you at the cemetery. I wish I had known both of them. I'm afraid I might have liked Mr. Eli best — you know I always fall easily

for those smart, sardonic young men. I like their banter, even though I sometimes think that is a very superficial reason to choose a beau.

2. I was shocked when I saw the date of Mr. Gabriel's death. He died so soon after you had wed. And when you told me that he had "fallen from the sky," when the surveillance balloon crashed, I could only think of you. You told me you were frightened every time he went up in the air, and then you had the courage to go up with him. In disguise! And what cruel irony that you received the news by telegram. And I know that Mr. Eli made you angry, wheedling and cajoling you into so many dangerous initiatives. But how wonderful to be with a man who has such confidence in you! (PS. I wish I had known Great-Grandfather Jules as well, but at least I have heard about him and have seen photographs. I am glad you two had a long and happy marriage, and I think kindly of him because you told him your truths and he married you. He measured your character with love and generosity.)

3. I think you are the most courageous person I know. This is a strange thing to say, because you have kept so many secrets for so many years, but you are also the most honest person I have known.

I confess to you that I am both excited and a

little scared about my own next adventure, serving in the Army. Though I have pooh-poohed all of mama and daddy's concerns about leaving home, crossing an ocean, and caring for people whose wounds are likely to be more terrible than what I have been trained for — you know my heart and my mind, and they are full of bravado. That is a very different thing than being really, truly brave. But now I know that there must be some of your courage and persistence running in my veins, and I feel…better. I will not disappoint you.

4. I realize that I don't know much about love, real love. Until now, I have judged young men on three criteria. Could they dance? Could they kiss? Could they make me laugh? Actually, come to think of it, I've not yet met a man who was good at all three. I hope I will someday! I will be guided by your story. If you don't have the courage to love the right person, then you don't deserve love at all.

And now, Granny Vic, I am going to take my frivolous, frightened-but-willing self to bed. But I could not sleep without telling you what you inspired in me.

All my love,
Alma

CHAPTER 24

VICTORIA'S JOURNAL, 1862

What is the measure of a good man? I have known good men: my brother, my father, kind doctors I have met in my work, those who did not care whether they cut away gray or blue uniforms, caring only for the man and his suffering. But I have been puzzled by what constitutes true goodness, true greatness of spirit in time of war, where winning is all and men seem like nothing but cannon fodder. But today, as the terrible battles of Fredericksburg ravaged people and place, word came to us of heroism and courage, exemplified in one modest Confederate sergeant, Richard Rowland Kirkland.

We have been overwhelmed with wounded at Chimborazo, and yet we know that the numbers of dead and wounded among the Union troops were far greater. As the Confederate wounded came to us, what I call "peacock-talk," the little-boy excitement of prevailing against great odds, ran around the hospital. But that talk quieted as the realities of wounds and a long, uncertain path to recovery took center stage. And then a quieter story, a glorious story, began to make the rounds on the ward about

Sergeant Kirkland. As I cared for one young man, cleaning and bandaging and trying to distract him from his pain, I asked him to tell me about the place he came from. He looked at me and then did exactly what I wanted, turning away from the sight of the inflamed and oozing site I was cleaning. "I come from the town where the Angel of Marye's Heights was born," he said proudly. "Flat Rock, South Carolina."

"I don't know about this Angel," I said. "You must tell me more."

And off he went, young Ezra from Flat Rock, telling me quite a tale. "Oh, it was a terrible, awful thing. I didn't know this part about soldiering, about listening to the moans and the cries of those men we had near-to slaughtered." He shuddered. "I used to help my daddy slaughter pigs, and you'd hear those pitiful grunts and squeals, as if they knew what was coming. Well, this," he swallowed hard, "was so much worse."

"Yes," I said, trying to keep a bitter note out of my voice, "I understand the system General Lee's lieutenants set up was near-perfect. Inescapable, even."

"You know, we had ourselves all lined up behind the stone wall that squats right at the bottom of Marye's Heights. There we all were, a wall ourselves: artillery, cavalry, everybody. One by one, we stretched for miles. Those dumb Yankees made their way across the canal, and then they set out toward us across a wide-open field. At first I was scared to death. But then I saw what was going to happen. As they came close to us, we mowed 'em down like tin soldiers. There was nowhere to hide! You would think that being dead was the worst thing that could happen." He gulped. "But it is not. Not a bit of it. The worst was laying in wait behind the stone fence, and listening to the sound of all those Union blues who were hit, but not dead. They were crying out for water, for their mamas, asking God to take them."

"Hold still one more minute," I said as I wrapped the last bandage and tucked the ends inside. He looked in amazement at the clean white strips obscuring his wound. "You're done?"

I nodded. He struggled up to a sitting posture, and I tucked a coarse pillow behind his back. "Finish telling me about the Angel," I said, "and then I have to see who else needs help."

He grabbed my hand. "You won't believe this. Sergeant Kirkland just couldn't listen to those Union boys crying out anymore. He marched right up to General Kershaw and asked if he could offer them some comfort. At first, I heard that Kershaw said no. But Kirkland just kept asking, and I guess because they come from the same county, General Kershaw finally gave in and told him he could go over the wall and see what he could do."

I perched on the edge of young Ezra's cot and took his hand. His face was white with exertion, trying to tell his story and do his fellow soldier justice. "Kershaw told him he might be shot, but I guess Kirkland said he would take his chances. So he filled up a bunch of canteens with water and stepped out onto the battlefield. He went from man to man with water, and then he came back to our line and took some clothing and blankets." Ezra shook his head. "For a long time, he went back and forth, back and forth."

"And no one fired a shot?" I asked.

"Not a one."

"How old is Sergeant Kirkland?"

"Year older than me. Nineteen."

That night, when I finally fell into bed, too tired to remove anything but my boots, I could not stop thinking about the "slaughterhouse" imagery young Ezra had conjured. I thought of my long days and nights, cleaning, bandaging, coaxing dying men to have a little lukewarm broth, cleaning up from one amputation after another. That night I made my decision. Nursing alone was like being on a waterwheel. We just kept coming back to the same wretched place, a place of dying men, ruined families, sometimes brother against brother, and the wheel would turn and we would start all over again.

I fell asleep and dreamed of Courage. In my dream, the Angel of Marye's Heights was riding my horse. Horse and rider cantered up to the split-rail fence outside the hospital where Courage was usually tied up. The Angel dismounted and held out his hand to me. I reached out to take his hand and he began to fade away, a little bit at a time. But I heard him say, "You and Courage, you should be getting yourselves into some trouble, my friend. It is time."

CHAPTER 25

VICTORIA'S JOURNAL, 1862

She is a fearsome and fearless teacher, Mrs. Greenhow. On each visit after Eli's introduction, ostensibly paying her a call out of compassion and concern for her young daughter, I learn something new.

I would bring ribbons with me to braid in Little Rose's hair. She would stand at my side, and I would brush the tangles out of her tresses, and then Mrs. Greenhow and I would visit, trading tales, as women do, about our families, our favorite foods, no longer available in time of war, and even our thoughts on women's fashion.

Hairstyles were of particular interest. The guard who was always standing nearby, barely listening to our highly unexciting female chatter, found our conversations mystifying.

"I don't know how you ladies can find so much to discuss about hairdressing," he would say. We would turn our blank countenances to him, smile distractedly, and return to our work.

Of course, it was work indeed, disguised by our seemingly empty-headed trading of local gossip and fashion.

Rose's access to paper and pen was very limited, since the guards felt sure she was writing coded secrets and looking for ways to smuggle what they considered traitorous information out of the Old Capitol Prison. Indeed she was, as her many conquests in the Union government worshipped at her altar. So skillfully did Rose share information she'd gleaned that Union security became as leaky as a sieve. One day Rose asked the pink-faced young guard if she could try a new hairdo on me. He narrowed his eyes at her, swept his gaze to me, then back to Rose. She tilted her head, whisked her fan once or twice, and said, "Oh, Sergeant, it is so sultry out here in the yard. I think that Miss Cardworthy would be so much more comfortable if we could get her beautiful hair rolled right up on top of her head."

The young sergeant stammered another objection or two. Rose beckoned him closer. "Now, Sergeant, you know that the Bible says a woman's hair is her crowning glory. All I want to do is take very good care of Miss Cardworthy's crowning glory. And you," she said, with a conspiratorial tap of her fan on his hand, "will have first look at the beautiful nape of her neck that will be revealed." She leaned closer to Sergeant Pink Cheeks and whispered, "You know, she is renowned for the beauty of her neck. She is a…" She hesitated, seemingly searching for the right word, and then she lit up. "She has a neck like a swan, and I think you are going to enjoy that sight like no other today." She turned to me. "Miss Cardworthy, if Sergeant Ames allows us the privilege of carrying out my vision for your elegant hair-style, will you allow him to admire your neck?"

I pretended to think the matter over. "I believe I will. But no touching."

He blushed. "You ladies talk circles around me, Mrs. Greenhow."

She laughed. "Now Sergeant, will you be kind enough to bring me my scissors? I am going to show Miss Card-worthy a wonderful trick with some ribbons, but I need to make a few snips here and there."

Poor Sergeant Ames. He was lost before the battle had begun.

And after delivering the scissors, with what was surely meant to be a stern admonishment that he would be col-lecting them as soon as Mrs. Greenhow was done, he set-tled himself on a bench to watch the proceedings.

For the next hour, Mrs. Greenhow gave me a brisk les-son in concealing notes in the carefully rolled and twisted coils of hair. As we sat in plain view of poor, addled Ser-geant Ames, she used ribbons as stand-ins for notes and showed me how to conceal anything — a note, a map — in my hair.

Ames, however, was not quite as dim as he appeared. "Mrs. Greenhow," he called out, when asked to admire my completed coiffure, "I don't understand. You can't see the ribbons at all, they're completely hidden. What's the point of ribbons no one can see?"

But of course, Rose had an answer. "Oh, dear Sergeant,

that is the mystery and the pleasure of this hairstyle. The only one who sees Miss Cardworthy's...ribbons will be her lover. He will unfurl each coil, gently, gently, and find the gift of a ribbon in each one. A secret gift — just for him. Along, of course, with any other...surprises Miss Cardworthy chooses to share."

Ames's pink cheeks turned scarlet. "Oh...oh," he stammered. "Of course." He looked down at the ground, anywhere not to meet our eyes.

Rose stood and laid her hand on his cheek. "Dear Sergeant, I fear you might have a fever. Your face is burning hot."

"I'm fine, just fine, ma'am. But perhaps I will fetch a jug of cold water for us all."

"Oh, that is a marvelous idea," said Rose. "You want to be cool and refreshed while you admire Miss Cardworthy's beautiful swan neck."

And off he went, leaving just enough time for Rose to pluck a knitting needle from her sewing bag and scratch the beginning of her cipher key in the dirt.

"Next month," she whispered, "my sources tell me the commander wants to send me away. You must come again each week so that we can finish the cipher before I am gone."

CHAPTER 26

MAGGIE
OXFORD

When Beau and I returned from our walk, Michael and Phoebe were still dawdling over breakfast. The day's papers — the Memphis *Commercial Appeal, The Wall Street Journal,* and *The New York Times* — had been dismantled and distributed. Michael had possession of all the sports news, and Phoebe was completing the crossword puzzle in ink, as is the tradition in our family. Michael always points out that it's not because we get everything right, it's just because we're an arrogant bunch.

"What news from town?" asked Phoebe.

"Not much," said Beau. "Oh, I'd say that Missy Weaver's trip to Memphis was cosmetic in nature."

Phoebe raised her eyebrows, "Really? I thought she had given all that up after the case of the misaligned ears during her last disappearing act to Memphis."

I was puzzled. "Beau, did I miss something? I don't remember speaking to anyone named Missy Weaver this morning."

Beau shook his head. "It's all the art of observation, honey. You're not the only detective in the family."

"Merciful God," said Michael. "I cannot deal with

another sleuth."

"I've got it!" I said. "Tall, skinny blonde in leopard leggings? Sunglasses and a big hat."

"That's Missy," said Phoebe tartly. "I think she's spending every last penny of her late husband's estate on foolishness and vanity."

"Easy for you to sound so superior, Mrs. Cardworthy," said Beau. "You were beautiful the day I met you, and you're even more beautiful today."

"Foolishness," said Phoebe. "We are all as God made us and that should be the end of it." She considered for a moment. "Well, except for finding an extremely skilled colorist, of course. The Bible says a woman's hair is her crowning glory." I reached for the orange juice pitcher. Where had I just heard that expression? And then I remembered...Victoria's journal.

Michael put down the local sports page and made a frowny face. "I've always thought we could live in your town, Beau. But there's not enough sports coverage in any of these papers. How do you live with that kind of deprivation?"

"Good thing there's twenty-four-seven ESPN," I retorted. "I'm sure there's some compelling track and field event in Perth or East Jesus, Texas, and I'm sure ESPN is covering it." I saw Michael ready to protest and segue into his longstanding, ever-expanding soliloquy on why all news should be sports news; when last I heard that particular speech it had something to do with stock market movement, the consumer price index, hemlines, and tattoos. Or wait, was it waistlines and wigs and the perennial favorite, wardrobe malfunctions? I decided to cut him off before a stem-winder took wing.

"Beau, I have one big question. Now, we know that Victoria was a spy, but here's what I don't understand. Was it for the Confederacy? Or for the Union? I'm still not sure. I know Rose Greenhow taught her all those spycraft skills, and Rose was an unrepentant Confederate booster. But somehow it seems that Victoria must have worked for the Union side, given her relationship with Gabriel. Doesn't that make sense?"

"Well, Gabriel was a free man by the time the war got under way, so aside from fellow feeling for those of his people who were enslaved — and I'm sure he felt that — you have to remember, he didn't have a personal dog in that fight. But what you ask is an interesting question. The reality was that many of the medical staff members — whether they were in a Confederate or Union hospital — treated whatever soldiers came their way. I don't know what created that culture — maybe the Hippocratic Oath or just the decency of people who were willing to care for others. From the staff lists I've been able to locate from the hospitals, Victoria certainly started in a Confederate hospital."

"Chimborazo in Richmond, right?"

"Exactly."

"So if she did switch to the Union side — for her work in Armory Square and maybe other hospitals and, perhaps, in espionage as well — when did she do that? And why? And wouldn't she have been a figure of suspicion? And what about Eli Mays? I still don't know why Victoria married him."

"Those are all reasonable questions, Maggie," said Beau. "And I can suggest ways you might be able to find answers, but this is why genealogical research is so slow. Every question can take you in many directions. It is slow, taxing, meticulous work, honey."

I thought of how we'd made fun of Uncle Beau over the years for clipping and keeping all those brittle, pee-colored newspaper articles, and for his room-size wall charts that chronicled the Cardworthy births, deaths, marriages, divorces, and, of course, our favorite, the footnoted scandals.

"I know how hard you've worked on all this, Beau. I'm just a spoiled brat wanting to learn everything right away — but you've always been the gentleman with the answers."

Beau shook his head. "Well, sometimes I think I was answering questions nobody had asked."

"Okay, now I'm asking," I said. "Project one: Is there some kind of online record about the staff in the Union hospitals?"

"Better than that. There's a record, all right, and it is online, so I downloaded it and printed it out for the years we know from the journals that Victoria was working as a battlefield nurse and then a hospital nurse — so from mid-1861 to about 1864."

"She stopped before the war ended?"

"Indeed she did. She went to prison in 1864, though as it turned out, she continued working as a nurse, caring for fellow prisoners. She actually had a fair amount of latitude to move around the Old Capitol Prison."

"They treated her like a 'trusty,' " I said.

"A trustee? Like a member of the board?" asked Phoebe.

Beau patted her check. "You are such an innocent, darlin'. T R U S T Y," he spelled. "That's what inmates are called if they are considered trustworthy. And they get special privileges and responsibilities."

"And," I pointed out, "you know where the term was first used? Right here in Mississippi in the early 1900s, at Parchman Farm, because the prison was supposed to be self-supporting and even generate some profits. So instead of a full staff, they used inmates they could trust. The most privileged were the 'trusty shooters,' equipped with shotguns to keep guard on the other inmates."

I was just getting warmed up, but the room had grown silent.

"Let me answer the question you're all wondering about," said Michael. "I have no idea how a woman who cannot understand the most basic geometry of properly loading a dishwasher can learn and retain all this arcane stuff."

"Women defenders," I said. "You know, those gals I worked with during the Limousine Lothario case? They taught me all sorts of interesting...history."

"Well done, Maggie," said Beau. "I like a girl who knows a lot. That's why I married your Aunt Phoebe."

"Yes," muttered Michael. "But Phoebe can load a dishwasher, too."

CHAPTER 27

MAGGIE
OXFORD

It was 10 a.m., Beau and I were well fortified with coffee, and we managed to persuade Phoebe and Michael that we needed all hands on deck. The four of us climbed two flights of stairs in Phoebe and Beau's house to the attic, which had been converted to a combination girls' dormitory and playroom. "Five granddaughters," I said as we opened the door. "I can't imagine what the giggle factor must be in this room when they're all in town visiting."

"You know, I miss a lot of that," said Phoebe. She perched on the window sill and straightened a few stray teacups on the kid-size table. "I miss all the tea parties and oh, my, how those girls could talk, talk, talk, and probably tell me things I had no right to know."

"Really?" I said. "Those little granddaughters would reveal their secrets to you?"

"Theirs, and sometimes I'd hear things I probably shouldn't have heard about their mamas and daddies. But they knew I could keep a secret." Phoebe made the universal zip-the-lip gesture to seal the deal.

"Speaking of secrets," said Michael, "is that what brought us to the inner sanctorum of little-princess-land up here?"

"You bet," said Beau. "Where better to hide family secrets than in the attic?"

Beau sat on the edge of one of the beruffled twin beds and pulled off his shoes. Then he stood on the bed, stretched up, and pulled on a rope. A set of wooden stairs came down, landing neatly right next to the bed.

"Okay," said Michael. "Just tell me what I'm looking for, I'll go up and get it. I'd just as soon not see you climb up that little stairway to heaven."

Beau protested, but Michael prevailed.

"Big red boxes," said Beau, "the kind that have those little nooks for storing ornaments after Christmas." Michael docilely accepted Beau's offer of a head strap equipped with a miner's light.

"You look exactly like an extra in *How Green Was My Valley*," I volunteered. "Very Welsh miner in the dark."

Michael ignored me and disappeared into the dark. We stood underneath the entrance to the attic, looking up as if we were watching for meteor showers — or expecting the roof to fall in. Several thumps and a few expostulations later, he reappeared in the opening.

"Lots of those red boxes," he said. "Which ones do you want?"

"We're looking for the one that says 'Hospitals, 1861 to 1865,' " said Beau. "And be careful. Once in a while a critter gets in there and makes a nest. You don't want to step on something, dead or alive."

Michael mumbled something unintelligible. "Couldn't hear ya!" called Beau. In a few moments, I heard a cheerier sound. Michael thumped his way back to the opening, and slowly his body re-emerged, feet, legs, torso, and arms — holding a dusty red box.

We had a few minutes of drama while Phoebe spread an old sheet on one of the beds to protect the ruffles from the dust. Then Beau lifted the lid and we all peered inside and saw yellowing folders, stacked in two rows, each holding equally yellowed, brittle papers.

One row was labeled Confederate Hospitals; the other Union.

"Here we go," said Beau, cheerfully. "I knew there was a reason to save all these documents."

"And exactly what are they?" asked Michael.

"What we were talking about — staff lists from the most important hospitals."

"Can I look inside the folders?" I asked Beau.

"Of course, of course, honey — that's why we got 'em down. We're going to do a little primary-source research project — well, these are copies of primary documents, but still, they've been in the attic long enough to be historic themselves!"

Phoebe did the long-suffering-spouse daily double: an eye roll, followed by a sigh. "Let's take all this mess outside. It's a beautiful day, and we can shake that dust into the yard."

Thanks to Victoria's journal, we knew exactly when she left Chimborazo. With the Union lists, we'd be able to figure out when she began her work at Armory Square Hospital. A great theory, but the reality was a little daunting: pages and pages of names written in an endless variety of faded, spidery handwriting.

"Didn't anyone ever print?" I whined.

Michael fixed me with a glance. "Let's remember you're the jefe of this little project. The rest of us are just unpaid labor."

"Now, now," said Phoebe. "This is kinda fun. I love seeing all these beautiful, Spencerian hands."

We'd divided the Union records into four equal stacks, concentrating on those with dates that overlapped the period after Victoria left Chimborazo for good, and when — we assumed — she'd begun her espionage career, passing information about Confederate troop movements, the condition of the troops, and whatever she could glean about future plans. And on we went, painstakingly going through the lists of names. We found Victorias, all right, plenty of them, and even a few Almas, Victoria's middle name — but no Victoria Alma Cardworthy or Victoria Alma Mays, assuming that she changed her name when she married Eli Mays in 1863.

By 1 p.m., we'd gone through all the lists and all the names. Nothing. "Well," said Phoebe, "what about lunch at Lamar Lounge? That'll perk us all up."

I think of Lamar Lounge as a bar — with food. Good food, mind you, but bar food. There's a giant *The Good, The Bad and the Ugly* movie poster next to the bar, inexplicably in French. And there's a patio out back, with experts tending what is claimed to be the "only pit-smoked, whole-hog barbecue in Mississippi."

And so there we were in a twinkling, and Phoebe was correct — we were greatly cheered a half hour into ribs and some sides. The Mississippi caviar was good, but not quite as good as Phoebe's. I told her so. "Oh, thank you, darlin'. I think so, too, but...." She looked around and lowered her voice, "I don't want to hurt anyone's feelings." Still, we managed to polish off every last bite of the caviar and everything else. It's a quixotic operation, Lamar Lounge, because all the profits get distributed to Mississippi nonprofit groups. So the more you eat, the more good karma you generate. At least, that's the theory.

On the way back home, I asked Phoebe and Beau to drop me off at the Square. "I'll walk back. I have eaten myself into a stupor *again*."

"Want company?" asked Michael. I saw him sneak a look at his watch, and he saw me catch him.

"What's on?"

"Oh, you know, just a little Sunday football."

"I'm good. I might wander through Square Books again and find something for the boys."

The autumn sun was already cooling, but after generating all that heat with all that food, I was glad to take a brisk walk around the square. Mr. Faulkner's bench called me once again, and I settled in to watch as everyone who'd had a late, post-church lunch came out of restaurants around and off the square. Families, college students with their visiting parents, grandparents holding hands. *Is life really this idyllic here?* I wondered.

Something about those hours of going through names, looking for the Victoria needle in the haystack, was bothering me. I kept thinking we had missed something — where was Victoria? We knew she'd been at the Armory — she mentioned it several times in her journal. But why wasn't her name there?

And then, filled with lunch and seduced by the late afternoon sun, I feel asleep on Mr. Faulkner's bench.

I woke with a start when someone touched my shoulder. Disoriented and embarrassed, I shook the hand off and began spluttering. "Oh, I'm fine, I...I —"

Michael stood there, grinning at me. "And you make fun of me for falling asleep in the third quarter of football?"

"Go away," I said. "I'm thinking."

Michael sat down next to me and pulled me to him. "*Cara*, what's wrong? I was only teasing you."

"I just keep thinking about Victoria — about how lonely she must have been. Leading all sorts of hidden lives — married to Eli Mays, but loving Gabriel — and how dangerous that was! And spying? Didn't people hang for that?"

Michael took my hands in his and faced me. "Maggie, whatever happened is done and gone, more than a century ago. There is nothing you can do right now, whatever happened to Victoria. And we know there was a happy ending to this story. Victoria fell in love — again — and married Jules. They're right there...." He turned and gestured up the hill at the cemetery. "They're together, and they had a wonderful life together, even if Jules did die young by today's standards. From all evidence and family stories, he and Victoria enjoyed very good lives. Without," he smoothed my hair, "direct interference from that troublesome great-great-great-granddaughter who surely would have wanted to meddle, if only she'd been born a few generations earlier."

I sat up indignantly. "I am not troublesome."

"Oh, you are. You've raised troublesome to an art form — but most of us enjoy it."

He stood up and held out his hand. "We're going to

have to head to the airport soon; we have little ruffians waiting for us. I'm sure they've already tortured Anya, and we need to rescue her. And if we stay here any longer, I'm going to have throw out all my clothes and start hanging out at the Big and Wide shop."

With the last of the sun in the western sky, we headed back to Phoebe and Beau's. "You know," said Michael, "Phoebe refers to us as her VIP guests. How often do you get called that?"

I laughed, and then I stopped. "That's it! That's what is bothering me."

"Being a VIP?"

"Better," I said. "Being a VAC — just like Victoria Alma Cardworthy's maiden initials."

CHAPTER 28

VICTORIA'S JOURNAL, 1863

"I will," I lied. The justice of the peace at the Oxford courthouse asked me if I would love, honor, and obey Mr. Eli Mays. I stood facing Eli, and I know he saw a telltale will o' the wisp look of confusion and pain cross my face.

"Courage," he had whispered to me as we had walked up the stairs to the courthouse. "This is the only way you, and he, can be protected." He offered his arm, and I gratefully slipped mine through his. Courage, indeed! To me, it felt as if I were behaving in cowardly ways, taking advantage of Eli to cover my tracks. His argument was that a married woman would not excite the same interest or curiosity as a single woman.

I knew he was right. Eli had offered to make me his wife, many times. I had always refused. But a week ago, I had awakened in the middle of the night, sick with dread. It was a cool night, but head to toe I was clammy with sweat. I tore off my wet nightgown and threw it across the room. I plucked a clean shift out of the bureau drawer and with trembling fingers, buttoned up and climbed back into bed. I wrapped a shawl around my shoulders and rolled my saggy childhood pillow into a kind of bolster.

"Enough of this paralysis!" I exclaimed to the empty room.

"Worry is useless. It is for cowards and dullards. You need a plan." There was no answer, of course, but I willed myself to simply be silent and listen. What did I want to happen? At first, there was nothing to hear. No voice, no counsel, no warning, not one word, fair or foul. I closed my eyes, I let go my fierce grasp on the shawl, and oddly, I felt the room grow warmer. It was still too far from daybreak to expect the sun to take away the chill. Instead, it felt as if some comforting hand was on my head. My mother's? Gabriel's? My brother's? In the silence, I knew exactly what I wanted, and no matter how impossible it might be, it was warming simply to know with clarity what should happen. I felt the knots in my neck and shoulders soften. I sat up straighter and opened my eyes. Still just me, alone in the bed, alone in the bedroom, with only a waning moon to send light through the window. "But I am not alone," I said, out loud. "I have books, I have friends, I have a sweetheart, I have...love." I reached over to the little two-drawer table my father had made for me, and plucked my writing board, my blue-ink pen, and a few sheets of clean foolscap from the drawer. I drew up my legs, bent at the knees, and settled the writing board and paper on my impromptu desk. I thought for a moment, and entitled the paper "The Declaration of Independence of Victoria Alma Cardworthy."

Half an hour went by in an instant as I dashed off my four points of independence. It was as if I was "spirit writing," as the crazy fortune-teller in Eli's favorite tavern does. No disconnect between thought and pen, all flowed together as if some stagnant fountain had come back to life and in its rejuvenation was bubbling only the freshest, the sweetest of water.

"Gabriel," I whispered. "Shall I read you what I've written?" I took the silence for yes, because I knew he was there with me, in that room, leaning on the window sill and looking out as the clouds drifted by the fading moon.

Declaration 1. I, Victoria Alma Cardworthy, am entitled to all that the masculine sex takes for granted: the right to travel, the right to earn and keep my own money, the right to vote, the right to have opinions and say them out loud.

Declaration 2. I am entitled to love whomever I choose. And if that gentleman loves me back, we are entitled to marry and live together as husband and wife.

Declaration 3. Although I am generally a law-abiding citizen, because the law does not treat me equally in any way (I nearly blotted the paper midnight blue in its entirety when I tried to emphasize "in any way"), I am entitled to circumvent certain restrictions and constrictions if I judge them foolish, cruel, or unreasonable.

Declaration 4. Because as a woman it is so difficult to lead the life I crave, I am entitled to....

I paused for a moment. What was it I was actually

entitled and able to do? I shook my head. The answer to that was "precious little." Undeterred, I finished the fourth declaration: I am entitled to make such adjustments, in behavior, in clothing, in disguising face and form, and in mission, to lead a life of meaning and consequence.

I folded my declarations carefully, tucked them under the pillow, and fell into a deep, dreamless sleep, the kind reserved for the innocent and the just. It is unlikely many would consider that sleep deserved, but when I awakened, I could see a path ahead through Dante's dark wood.

CHAPTER 29

VICTORIA'S JOURNAL, 1864

When I was five years old, the mayor's wife had twins, a boy and a girl. It's not that there weren't other twins, even in our small town. It's just that I had never met any before. Everything about twins was mystifying and exciting to me. It seemed like a miracle: two babies, born at the same time. And even though they looked alike when my mother and I went to pay a call, very red in the face, wiggly, and wrinkled like crumpled-up paper, I could see differences right away. The little girl kept moving her head all around as if she were looking for something she'd lost. The little boy threw his hands over his head as if he were waving, two-handed, at friends out in the world.

Because they didn't have room in the crib for two babies, I remember that a hired man who helped out around the mayor's place hammered together a big, square wooden box, like a dresser drawer. It was dark, beautiful wood. Mahogany, my mama told me. Jeb, the man who made the box, then sanded gently curved rocker boards so they were smooth as the silk on my church dress. Jeb trimmed the outside of the box with long, thin boards with fancy loop-de-loop carving. Funny, how names stick with you. I'll never forget Jeb's name, because when you would ask how he was, he would always say, "I'm Jeb with a job so every day is a good one."

When the improvised double cradle was ready, Mama and I brought over lots of soft quilts. Mama was Oxford's reigning queen of the jelly-roll quilt, so that was the baby present we brought when that big rocker box was ready.

The babies, named Cara and Giovanni, because their mama had come to Oxford, Mississippi, all the way from Genoa, Italy, looked a little prettier than the first day I'd seen them. They weren't as red as a watermelon anymore, and their skin wasn't wrinkly at all.

I got to hold Giovanni on my lap for a few minutes. I still remember how important I felt, and how Giovanni tried to wiggle even closer to me. I said, "Mama, I think he likes me!"

My mama bent over the two of us and said, "You're doing a fine job, Victoria. And he already knows you're a girl child. He's nestling in just in case you're old enough to feed him." The ladies in the room all chuckled, but the twins' daddy blushed, and said, "I'll leave you ladies to your work."

Cara's mother, Mrs. Mayor (for that is how I thought of her), put her in the box. And then my mama lifted Giovanni and tucked him in right beside his twin. And I watched as the tiny hand she was waving around somehow found its way to Giovanni's arm. And although now I know she was much too young to have control of her movements, something amazing happened. She turned her face toward her brother, and her wandering little hand simply rested on his arm. Almost in an instant, both babies fell asleep, linked by touch, already deeply connected outside the womb, as they had been within.

Sometimes I dream about those twins, so connected that, as they grew, they would finish each other's sentences. And I think about my virtual twin, Virgil Alexander Cranston, and wonder if I could conjure him up again if I wanted. If I had to.

Virgil Alexander Cranston was my made-up Giovanni, a lookalike version of myself: a man, not a woman, imbued with freedoms no contemporary of my sex could enjoy.

Becoming Virgil was how I could pursue my goals: to melt into the Confederate ranks, to gather information and plans, and then to pass intelligence along to Gabriel, who could telegraph what I uncovered to officers in the Union army. Was I betraying my family? My brother, Jeremiah, was safely out of uniform, no longer useful as a soldier, thank God! I was tired of this war; every day it seemed to grind even those who survived into smaller, weaker versions of themselves.

Eli was right. Spies may be despised, may be considered treasonous and betrayers, but while those lofty principles of patriotism and commitment to the cause are invoked, people are still dying. If knowledge, because that is what spies gather, will help, then it is worth the moral compromise.

Loving Gabriel had changed me. I have no idea how I managed to hear his voice and know, immediately, that this man was for me, and I was for him. How foolish, how impetuous that sounds! I have confided in only two people, my brother, Jeremiah, and my friend Mr. Whitman. Jeremiah was more distressed than I had anticipated. "He will be murdered, Victoria, if people find out. And you may be in great danger as well. Mother and Father could not bear that sorrow. You must end this…friendship, for their sake, if not for yours."

"I had hoped you would understand, Jeremiah," I said. "You know what it is to love so wildly that you cannot imagine a life apart. I have seen you and Elizabeth. You are each individuals, but you are joined in every cause and every challenge." I paused for a moment. "Except, perhaps, when the Queen of Nosiness, Elizabeth's mother, comes to visit."

Jeremiah shook his head. "These are not joking matters, Vic. Elizabeth and I have known each other since we were children. Ours is an entirely different situation." Jeremiah reached for his crutch and pulled himself to a standing position.

"Mother and Father knew each other for seven months when they got married," I said tartly. "Time is not the arbiter of all successes."

Jeremiah reached out his arm, beckoning me to come embrace him. I came quickly to his side, and as he held me, it felt as if we were holding each other up.

"I think I understand, Vic. I know what it is to be crazy in love. When I almost died, you badgered me to stay alive for Elizabeth, and my dog, and so I did. I am just frightened for you, and for this man you love. I think you are so impatient to see a different world that you forget what it is to live every day in this one."

"That," I said, "is exactly why Victoria Alma Cardworthy is going to disappear for a while."

CHAPTER 30

VICTORIA'S JOURNAL, 1863

Turning from Victoria to Virgil was surprisingly easy. The curse of being the tallest girl in school instantly turned into a blessing. My broader-than-most-female's shoulders had gobbled up extra fabric when my mother made me dresses from the time I was a child, but now, it was easy for Eli to divert a Confederate soldier's garb my way. As a young man, I looked...mercifully unworthy of notice.

Cropping my hair, of course, gave me pause. I had always been vain about the abundance of red curls that defied taming or braiding, but there was something wonderfully light and free about not having to untangle at the end of each day, or to wear out my arms and my patience skewering all those heavy curls into a knot on the top of my head, or using hairpins to shape a more elegant bun at the nape of my neck. I realized the drastic haircut put paid to all Mrs. Greenhow's training on curls as hiding places for vital information, but the opportunities accorded me as Virgil rather than Victoria outweighed all other considerations.

How ironic it was that I never felt more womanly than when I was disguising myself as a man! With each step of my transformation, somehow I became more and more aware of how loving Gabriel, and being loved by him, made me acutely conscious of my spirit, and my body. I remembered our every encounter, and how both deliberate and wild I felt as we touched each other. Deliberate, because I knew love for the first time, and nothing felt wrong or out of bounds. Wild, because even the smallest touch, from the first moment we shook hands, made my knees nearly buckle. We were…together for the first time before we were married. I confessed to Gabriel that I was not a virgin; Eli had teased and tempted me into sexual congress when we were both fifteen. I was curious, of course, and Eli knew how to enchant and wear down an independent young woman. In addition, Mother and Father were so accustomed to me disappearing into the woods that although they lectured me, they had grown weary of trying to keep track of where I went and who I saw. And, they were grateful to Eli for escorting me home from school, offering what they saw as protection.

But my dalliance with Eli was simply that, nothing more. Although, of course, as we grew older, I knew that he had feelings for me. And while our experimentation was enjoyable, and while Eli knew a great deal for a very young man, that experience paled next to my feelings for Gabriel.

Oh, feelings! They were everything to me. I was drunk with love, craving Gabriel's hands and lips and those arms that could sweep me off Courage and into a lover's embrace. I began to understand the irresistible draw of a drug. As my patients grew dependent and frantic about morphia, so I found myself craving Gabriel. In the woods, in his sister's house when she was away, in a hidden bend in the river...I grew to understand how desperation leads to foolish risks.

One summer day we had gone to our favorite secret swimming hole. We were floating in the river, Gabriel on his back, enfolding me, as we both looked up into the cloudless sky, when we heard the snap of a branch breaking. In an instant, we were out of the water. Gabriel stood in front of me. A man emerged from the thicket, his rifle cradled in his arms.

"Let me see who you're hiding, boy," he said.

Gabriel stepped forward, "I was taking advantage of this woman. And I am heartily ashamed."

"She does not look as if she is trying to get away from you." He gestured to me. "Come here."

"No," said Gabriel, detaining me. "This is between you and me, sir. This woman is blameless."

"Let me go," I said to Gabriel, as coldly as I could.

I walked directly to the man. "How can I thank you, sir?"

He looked me over, puzzled but intrigued. My undergarments were completely soaked and pasted like sheer wallpaper to my body. I tentatively reached out a hand to him. Behind me I heard Gabriel's breath, quickening.

He took my hand. "I am sorry to be so...in disarray and so wet," I said. "But I would count it a favor if I could offer a chaste kiss in gratitude for your kindness."

"Right after I tie up this nigger."

"Oh," I protested, as I slipped my arms around his waist. "I am so cold, right to the bone. Will you warm me for a moment first? Then I will help you with the tying up." I looked over my shoulder. "He's not going anywhere," I said, with contempt.

His free arm encircled me, my mouth found his, as un-chastely as possible. I could feel his body stirring. And then, in an instant, I snatched the rifle from his loosening grasp. His face flushed red with rage.

"Stand down, sir," I said. "I will shoot you."

He looked at me, he looked at Gabriel, and he started toward me. I kept my word.

In a matter of moments, we had dressed and I was astride Courage. We were both weeping; we were both trembling; but we did what we had to do. And we never returned to the swimming hole again.

I am a murderer. But when Gabriel was in danger, I fought with what I had. I do not expect to be forgiven for what I did in this life or the next one. But I am at peace.

CHAPTER 31

VICTORIA'S JOURNAL, 1863

Eli visited to regard my disguise and to weigh in on the sight of me in a Confederate cavalry uniform, somewhat grander and more colorful than the infantry garb. Our wedding rings gave him privileges to come and go as he pleased at Mrs. Marshall's boarding house. "Now, Virgil," said Eli, waving his hand in a circle like an impresario. "Take a turn around and let me look at all aspects of you."

I turned slowly to accommodate his scrutiny.

"Not bad," he said. "You look quite…unremarkable." He came close to me and put his hands flat on my chest. I refused to flinch. He smiled, and took a step back. "And how have you made your womanly shape disappear?"

"I'm a nurse," I said brusquely. "Strong, strapping bandages are useful even when one is not injured."

"Nicely done."

I regarded myself in the glass, and the two rows of shiny buttons glinted back at me. "You men talk about women's vanity," I said, "and I give you this silly, furbelowed cavalry uniform as exhibit one that men are true peacocks at heart." I found the whole ensemble a little silly: bright yellow trim

on pants and coats, with officers adding a yellow sash. "Eli?"
I said, when he didn't answer. But he was all business now
and had more orders to issue. "You have to do something
about your complexion, Vic. You are too fair, and your skin
is too delicate."

His mandate to me was to ride Courage every day, hat-
less and gloveless, and sure enough, within a few weeks,
the skin on my face had darkened and lost its smoothness,
and I had calluses on my hands. Of course I could not conjure a beard, but as Eli pointed out, "Soldiers are rarely a
clean lot, and if you are not so scrupulous in your toilette,
the dust and dirt will hide the fact that there are no whisk-
ers sprouting." Together, we had decided that if I gave my
age as sixteen, no one would look too closely at the face of
a tall young cavalry volunteer, not yet in his full manhood
and hence not yet whiskery and coarse.

Courage was my trump card. The Confederate cavalry ranks were diminishing, and since I was joining up as
a mounted soldier, I brought not only myself but a fine,
healthy horse to this adventure. I knew he would draw
more attention than I would, and that suited me down to
my high boots.

April 10, 1863, was the date we settled upon for my
debut as a Confederate soldier. Through Eli's always useful connections, I was accepted into the First Brigade of
the North Carolina Cavalry as a volunteer enlistee, wearing gray and yellow but working for blue. Eli's sources
predicted a series of fierce battles coming, as the Union's

promising Fighting Joe Hooker rallied his exhausted forces and began to plan an assault against General Lee's Army of Northern Virginia. The day I made my way to the front was April 29, Jeremiah's twenty-third birthday, and with Gabriel's help and willingness to send contraband telegrams on my behalf from time to time, I was able to get my good wishes to Jeremiah on his actual birthday. "May be out of touch dear brother. Traveling to new post soon. Worry not, will be near old friends, the Chancellors. Yours V." Meanwhile, Lee was now welcoming all recruits, dismissing details of birthplace, experience, or history. I had been welcomed into my cavalry brigade, a volunteer unit, led by Brigadier General Wade Hampton. The Confederates were sixty-two thousand strong, but Hooker's largesse (he brought onions and potatoes for all, we heard) and his energy had revived the crushed spirits of his troops, and their numbers were growing daily.

On April 30, I saddled up with my fellow cavalrymen, and we began our progress toward the Chancellorsville Wilderness. We passed George Chancellor's handsome redbrick house, and I fastened my gaze on the upstairs windows, hoping to catch a glimpse of the girls who had been my playmates as children and friendly competitors at dances for the most handsome partners as we made our debuts as young ladies within months of each other. But all was dark and quiet at the home that had once seemed so familiar to me, and I turned face forward as the sky darkened, marching with my fellows into the bracket and bramble of

the Chancellorsville wilderness. Rumors were that Hooker's men were crossing the Rappahanock that very evening,
and I thought again how silly this all seemed: Johnny Reb
and Billy Yank marching blindly into darkness.

CHAPTER 32

MAGGIE
UP IN THE AIR

"*The Red Badge of Courage,*" I said to Michael. He ignored me. He was in his classic airplane mode. We'd boarded in Memphis and settled in our favorite configuration — Michael on the aisle, me in the window, *no one* in the middle seat. He'd eaten his peanuts and mine and was savoring some dark, malty brew and working his way through a complex gift agreement on his laptop. When I first heard that expression — "gift agreement" — I pictured Santa, surrounded by warring factions of children and elves, wisely adjudicating the issues that resulted in better contents for everyone's stockings. Of course, it's not nearly that interesting. Just a lot of legal back and forth so donors are recognized appropriately without hog-tying the beneficiary into naming a building after a horse or something, in perpetuity. "Planet Earth to Legalandia."

Michael sighed and looked up from his laptop "We're not on planet Earth, we are up in the air, that's number one, and number two, I'm really busy, figuring out how to demonstrate the many beauties of an irrevocable trust."

"Sounds dreadful. I've been reading about the Battle

of Chancellorsville, which was the first time Victoria/ Virgil was in combat — and General Lee's greatest triumph."

"That blowhard Hooker led the Union troops, right?" Here's what I love about my husband. I knew he'd rather get right back into charitable-foundation machinations, but he's such a geek about learning stuff, I can usually seduce him away from his legal minutiae for at least a few minutes.

"Right. Hooker thought it was going to be a walk in the park — his men were better fed, and he commanded almost double Lee's forces. But Hooker was a disaster — reorganizing, putting in new and mostly incompetent commanders, and then investing all his poor troops with an unfortunate sense that this was theirs to win. Wait, there's a perfect quote from him...." I flipped to the page I'd marked in the book Beau had lent me. "Here it is. Hooker says, 'My plans are perfect, and when I start to carry them out, may God have mercy on General Lee, for I will have none.' "

"It didn't turn out that way," said Michael.

"Nope. In the end, Hooker had to retreat back across the Rappahannock, and Lee's army was triumphant. Though there were heavy losses on both sides, and the Confederacy lost Stonewall Jackson, which was devastating to their cause."

"Can't remember. Was Jackson killed in battle?"

"No, that's the irony. He was shot by accident by his own men, when they ran directly into some Union troops at night and everyone just started firing in the dark — probably not the best strategy. Jackson's arm was amputated, and he was expected to live, but then he got pneumonia and died just a week or so later."

"Now I remember," said Michael. "And didn't they end up burying his arm in one location and the rest of him somewhere else? Or is that a myth?"

"Not at all. NPR did a story on it a few years ago. When Jackson's arm was amputated, it was on its way to being discarded on top of a pile of other severed limbs right outside the surgery tent."

Michael shuddered. "Yeah, I remember that awful scene in the Lincoln movie."

"Exactly. But everyone knew who Jackson was, and so the military chaplain decided to rescue his arm and give it a decent burial."

"Where?"

"At Ellwood Manor, not far from the hospital where Jackson had been treated. Big backstory on Ellwood Manor: William Jones built it around 1790 and grew grains and corn, kept slaves to get the work done, of course. Anyway, years go by, Jones's wife dies, and Jones grieves for five years. Then, he finds a way out of his sorrow. Now seventy-eight, but apparently still frisky, Jones marries Lucinda, his late wife's grand-niece, age sixteen. In his will, the old dude leaves both the houses — Ellwood Manor and their fancier place, Chatham Manor — to Lucinda, the young wife, on the condition that she doesn't remarry."

"Old guys! Such manipulative beasts," said Michael. "I can't wait till I'm old enough be one of those fine fellows."

"Good luck with that. I can't find even one manor in our real estate portfolio, never mind two. So anyway, the shameless old man and the lovely Lucinda did have one daughter, and when Lucinda finally decided she was going to defy Jones's wishes and remarry, that daughter inherited the houses. And when she fell in love, she married a schoolteacher named James Horace Lacy."

"How did we wander away from Stonewall Jackson's arm to Lucinda Lacy? I'm assuming she did take his name?"

"Indeed she did. But here's how we circle back to the beginning of the story. James Horace Lacy had a brother named Beverly Lacy. Jackson had recruited him to launch the chaplain corps in northern Virginia, and —"

"He's the guy who rescued Jackson's arm and had it buried," said Michael. "See I can still connect a few dots." He took a sip of his beer. "So where's the rest of Jackson?"

"Lexington, Virginia, in a place now known as the Stonewall Jackson Memorial Cemetery."

"And Virgil/Victoria was in the fray?"

"Appears so, though I couldn't find any details. But we know she wasn't listed as a casualty — and they were awful in number, more than thirty thousand. Here's a weird, terrible thing: Chancellorsville was considered the bloodiest battle ever fought in America — until a few weeks later, when Gettysburg's casualty toll was upward of forty thousand."

We both fell silent. The flight attendant came by. "Can I get you two another beverage?" In unison, we said yes. Beer for Michael, red wine for me. Michael looked at me. "I'm wondering...."

"What?"

"How soon can we register the boys as conscientious objectors?"

I shook my head. "I think that's a do-it-yourself job — the boys would have to register themselves. You know, I always start out on these pursuits thinking it will be interesting, I'll be solving some puzzle or problem."

"Is that what we're calling your 'unannounced sideline' — 'pursuits'? I'm more comfortable with something like, let's say, UMOs."

"I'll bite. I have no idea what a UMO is."

"Unauthorized Meddling Opportunity."

"Hey," I bridled, "sometimes people ask me to get involved."

"*Cara*, you invited yourself — and me — on this adventure."

"This is different! This is my family. Don't you want to know the family secrets?"

Michael sighed. "I'm going to go back to something safe like my gift agreement in a few minutes, but I think you need to consider what happens when secrets become public. Perhaps you've forgotten what it was like being in an unwelcome spotlight after our piddly little scandal went public."

"I'm sorry."

"Yeah, you've said that. What's the rest of your mantra?"

"I'm an idiot, I'm sorry, and I'll never be unfaithful again."

Michael nodded. "Excellent to hear you say it. Maybe half a dozen times a day would be instructive."

"I'll make a note of that. Anyway, secrets are mostly lousy, I think. They divide people into those who know and those who don't. It's like a bad riff on class warfare.

Information warfare."

Michael laughed. "You may have coined a phrase right there, little Miss-Let's-Reveal-All. And I know that all this information about Victoria is interesting. It's shocking, too. But I think you might ruminate about what Victoria might have wanted."

"I have. And you know what else? I think Beau had been ruminating about what Victoria would have wanted. Unconsciously, I think that's why he had Phoebe send me that photo, the one that makes me look like a long-lost twin of Victoria's. He wanted to start something, and he needed some help."

"And you were going to be his trusted Gal Friday in this discovery process?"

"Maybe. I don't know. But Beau takes this genealogy stuff very seriously. He's a scholar at heart, I think, and he wanted to share what he'd learned."

"He's a scholar, he's a gentleman, but he's also a Southerner, and I'm not sure how the rest of Victoria's descendants might welcome all these revelations."

"Why? Victoria was a hero!"

"Yes, we think she's a hero. But let's consider the facts of her life. She was a spy. She killed a man, admittedly to save Gabriel from certain death. She was a cross-dresser. She was married three times, once to a black man, defying miscegenation laws. And she quite likely endangered the lives of two of her three husbands."

"Eli, Gabriel, and then finally Great-Great-Great-Grandpa Jules. My grandmother Alma knew him, but he died long before Victoria did."

"And Victoria didn't marry again? Third time was

the end of the charm?"

"Guess so." I saw Michael's gaze creeping back to the laptop. "Go on," I said. "I didn't mean to take you away from philanthropic wheeling and dealing."

"Okay. But why were you talking about *The Red Badge of Courage* when you *first* interrupted me?"

"Oh, yes, Stephen Crane's novel. It was supposedly based on the Battle of Chancellorsville, even though Crane was born after the Civil War. I'd read it, but I'd forgotten what the red badge of courage was supposed to be."

"Blood, I'd guess," said Michael.

"Exactly right. So awful to think that's what young soldiers thought they needed to be a man."

I reached into the seat back pocket and fished out a tatty-looking copy of *The Red Badge of Courage*. "I'm reading it again. Used copy at Square Books — it called out to me, for two bucks."

And we both read our way home.

CHAPTER 33

VICTORIA'S JOURNAL, MAY 8, 1863
TWO DAYS AFTER CHANCELLORSVILLE

Despite the unexpected Confederate victory, so many of my fellow cavalrymen had been wounded or killed in Chancellorsville that those of us who were unmarked, and still had healthy mounts, were pressed into immediate service.

I volunteered to ride to Chimborazo and transport essential medicines back to the Wilderness Tavern–turned–hospital. Midway through my eleven-mile ride, I took cover in a heavily forested glen, stepped out of the clothes that had disguised me as Virgil, and unstrapped the bandages wound round my breasts, and in a twinkling, I was Victoria once again, complete with a bonnet to hide my shorn locks. Fear and hope motivated my surreptitious metamorphosis. Fear that my fellow nurses at Chimborazo would not be fooled by my masquerade, hope that coming as an old familiar friend would yield more information. At first, Courage didn't seem to notice the change at all. But as he felt the swirl of my skirts when I swung my leg across the saddle, he turned his head back to look at me, as if puzzling over what had happened.

I was uncertain what welcome I would receive at the pharmacy; despite the best efforts of the Rebel blockade-runners, its stores of drugs had been seriously depleted. Many of the hospital stewards and medical purveyors had been improvising, distilling their own drugs from medicinal herbs, and risking much to buy black market versions of medicines as they mysteriously became available.

Then, too, there was the uncertainty that roiled my stomach. I was a traitor, one way or another. I believed with all my heart that we had to end this terrible war, and that we had to put a stop to the madness of enslaving our fellow human beings. Yet as I walked the familiar corridors of Chimborazo, I inevitably encountered young men I knew: childhood friends, cousins, even patients I had cared for, who were now back in the hospital facing another round of recovery. Seeing them gave me vertigo. Whose side was I on? A Southern woman, a Northern sympathizer, in a love affair that was outside the bounds of all convention and law. Even after Chancellorsville and Lee's brilliant victory, from the inside it was easy to see that the Confederate troops were diminishing in front of our very eyes. And although the Rebel government was bleeding money, the rumors were growing that new resources might be at hand from the Russians, who were supporters of the Southern cause.

When I arrived at the medical dispensary with my list of requested medicines, I was greeted by an old friend, medical purveyor Horace Clemson. He took my hands in his and drew me into his office. "Miss Cardworthy, you are a welcome sight. When are you coming back to Chimborazo?"

"I do not know," I said, replying as candidly as I could. "Right now I am just trying to help restock supplies in the field hospital near Chancellorsville." I handed him my list, which was, I knew, overly optimistic and dreadfully long.

"That was a mighty victory and an even mightier surprise," said Clemson, running his finger down the list. "My, my. You're not asking for much, are you?"

"I am asking for *everything*. I know you understand what a field hospital looks like the day after a terrible siege."

Clemson sighed. "I do. Of course, there is more to come."

"And it is hard to call something a victory when both sides are losing so much. Don't you ever wonder...."

Clemson had turned his back to me, surveying his shelves of tinctures and drugs. Morphine, in its various forms, was the most highly prized; one of my patients called it "angel wings," because he said it took pain far, far, away, at least for a while.

Mr. Clemson turned back to me, holding a square wooden box that he had been filling with jars and stoppered flasks. "Don't I ever wonder what?"

"What is the point of all this?"

Clemson shook his head. "There is no point. The Yankees want what they want, and we want what we want."

"And what is it, exactly, that we want?" I said, unable to

keep the bitterness out of my voice.

"We want the right to govern ourselves as we see fit."

"Including the right to enslave others?"

Clemson carefully placed the wooden box on his high worktable.

"Miss Cardworthy, you seem unlike yourself. You have always been so willing to leap in and do what needs to be done. Have you..." he cleared his throat. "Have you developed concerns about the righteousness of our cause?" He asked in a neutral tone, but I suddenly realized once again how dangerous it was to speak at all freely. Exhaustion and fear were eroding my ability to stay focused.

I gestured at the chair near Mr. Clemson's worktable. "May I?"

"Of course," he said hastily, pulling it out for me. I sank into the chair gratefully.

"Thank you, thank you," I said. "I have not lost sight of our cause or the nobility of those who fight to protect the rights of all people to govern themselves." I took a deep breath. "If truth be told, I think I am just a little weary."

Clemson leaned against the table. "When is the last time you had something to eat or drink, Miss Cardworthy?"

I smiled. "That, Mr. Clemson, is an excellent question. And the answer is...I simply do not remember."

He leaned over and placed the back of his hand on my brow. I caught my breath; it was exactly the gesture my mother always used when she was worried one of us had a fever coming on.

"You are flushed," he said, "but not too warm." He took my hand and helped me to my feet. "Miss Cardworthy, I think you and I should cease our labors for just a short time and see what delights the officers' mess might provide."

Fortified by hearty, fragrant soup and crusty bread, both Mr. Clemson and I relaxed. "I must apologize," I said, "for my earlier remarks. But even though General Lee has exquisitely outwitted the Union in these last terrible days at Chancellorsville, from my vantage point, it appears that our brave Confederate boys are disappearing like dying leaves on a tree. It is spring," I said, looking out the window, and seeing beautiful dogwood and crape myrtle in bloom, "but on the fields and in the hospital, it feels like a cruel fall with a more dangerous winter to come." I reached across the table and put my hand on Clemson's. "It would be a kindness to let me know if you think I am overly concerned about the future."

He looked up from his bowl and tore a chunk of bread apart with far more vigor than was required. "You are not overly concerned. Here we are, the pride of the Confederacy's hospital. And yet, every day, I see us falling behind in so many ways."

"Tell me what worries you most."

"Not enough of anything and everything. The Union blockade is working better and better, and it keeps food, supplies, and medicines further and further out of reach. Many of our best physicians have left us, taken by disease, or exhaustion, or the pleas of their families to come home and help farm what is left of their lands. The ones we have now..." he trailed off, and shook his head. "Some are just very young, others have been pressed into service and are counting the days until they can leave these dreadful surgeries, others are simply drunks, landing in the military because it is the only job they can get."

"This is not the same heroic Chimborazo I remember," I protested.

"Nothing is what we remember," Clemson said quietly. "But that is just my little world of work and wounded. The news that comes in from the patients themselves is even worse. The Confederacy is bleeding money and men."

He pushed his bowl aside. "I have been here at Chimborazo since the start of the hostilities. Three years ago, men would come to us wounded, and they would start asking, right away, about when they could get back to their comrades. No matter how grievous the injuries, they were thinking about getting back." He leaned closer. "Now, it is entirely different, Miss Cardworthy. The men who came here from Chancellorsville should have been giddy with victory. The fact that our boys prevailed was a surprise to all, and a terrible blow to the Union. But despite their pride in what they have accomplished, most of what we hear is, 'When can I go home?' And I cannot blame them. They are exhausted, and they know that there is more of the same to come. And the Union forces are better fed, better clothed, and better armed, and they have reinforcements: men and horses."

A quizzical look came over Clemson. "How did you arrive here, Miss Cardworthy?"

"On Courage. The most loyal of friends. Why do you ask?"

His face seemed to turn circumspectly blank in an instant, as if an invisible washing cloth had strategically removed any hint of question.

"No reason in particular. I'm very happy you and Courage still have each other. Horses of his caliber are…rare treasures at this stage, and I'm sure there could be many calls on his service."

"Indeed. We are so happy, Courage and I, to be able to serve in our own small ways." Neither of us blinked. "After all," I said, with just a small edge of tartness in my voice, "Courage and I are carrying your medicines back to the field hospital."

We both stood. "Thank you for the soup and the company, Mr. Clemson."

He inclined his head in a gentleman's bow.

"I wish you…and Courage…all the best, Miss Cardworthy. I have valued our friendship for many years, and I have admired your extraordinary service in our hospital."

"My heart is in Chimborazo," I said. "It is difficult to come here, and it is even more difficult to leave."

"Ah, that solves a mystery," said Clemson. "Many of us had wondered where you kept that mysterious heart of yours."

I closed my eyes for just an instant and pictured Gabriel,

playing the "Prince of Denmark's March" in the woods. I thought of that Trumpet Voluntary and put a hand on the edge of the table to steady myself.

"You are you a music-lover, Mr. Clemson, are you not?"

"I am. But how did you know that?"

"I've often heard you humming in your dispensary, and I thought that music must bring you comfort and company for those long hours tending to your arsenal of medicines. What you called my mysterious heart just reminded me of a very beautiful piece of music, the 'Prince of Denmark's March.' "

"Ah, yes, the piece that's usually played on an organ with the trumpet stop engaged. Brides often fancy that piece of music."

"I am not a bride," I said hastily, "but I heard it played not too long ago on an actual trumpet; not the trumpet stop on the organ, but a real horn, and it was so pure, and so glorious."

"And where does the mystery enter the picture?" asked Clemson.

"How a piece of music that is more than 150 years old can feel as fresh as if it was composed that very moment by the person who is playing it. At least, that is how I heard the piece."

Clemson spoke as if he were choosing each word, one at a time. "Miss Cardworthy, that trumpeter must be very gifted, and very fortunate to have you as his audience." He cleared his throat. "Forgive my curiosity. You are perhaps keeping your news private, but I heard that you married recently. That is why I mentioned brides."

"You are correct. I married a childhood friend, someone I value very much. Sadly, though, my husband and I are not able to share a home yet. We are both called to service in this war."

"And he is a musician?"

"I do not catch your meaning."

"Ah, I assumed you married your...trumpeter."

"Oh, that is a long story for another time," I said. "Shall we return to your office so I can collect the supplies you've so kindly assembled for me? Those who are less fortunate than we are awaiting your healing medicinals."

CHAPTER 34

MAGGIE
OAKLAND

"Are we going to a wedding this month?"

Michael rolled over. "Beats me," he said. "Whose wedding?"

I stretched and tucked myself into the crook of his arm. "I don't know. I just woke up with wedding music in my head."

"Too late. We're already married."

"Oh, good. I couldn't deal with your mother or mine again over the tablecloths, the weird cousins, the rabbi, the priest, or the amount of skin a bride can or cannot show."

"I'm happy to say I've forgotten all that over the past seventeen years," said Michael.

"Isn't it heavenly to be in our own bed in our own house?"

"It is," he said. "With our own children and a molting cat and smelly dog and hot-and-cold-running Pac-12 sports available at the touch of the Harmony remote."

I groaned. "Please tell me there's not football on this very minute."

"College, not NFL," said Michael, craning his neck toward the nightstand, patting the surface methodically in a search for the remote.

There was a commotion outside the bedroom door, composed of equal parts clattering silverware and squabbling boys. "I've GOT it!" insisted Zach in a stadium-level stage whisper. "Just open the door."

"Are you nuts?" said Josh, "Jeez, they could be like naked or having sex or something. You've got to knock."

"Come in," I called. "Fully pajama-ed parents are in the house."

With that, the door banged open and Zach, careening only slightly, delivered a tray to the bed: a thermos of coffee, cream, sugar, two jelly jars of orange juice with the lids screwed on, and a tower of heavily buttered toast — rye for me, whole wheat for Michael. An empty yogurt cup held five dandelions. Their heads were bobbing and discharging seeds hither and yon.

"Nice work, guys," said Michael, dosing his coffee with cream and sugar. "I could get used to this."

I patted the side of the bed, "Hop on, you two, and tell us every single thing that happened while we were gone."

Zach's report: Anya had thrown Raider out of her bedroom once and for all, unable to withstand the unremitting incidents of flatulence. Lexie had come to see Josh five times — he brandished a small pad with hash marks on it, keeping score of his older brother's romantic encounters. And Anya had taken them for pizza and let Zach order two extra sides of anchovies to put on top. "She's the best," Zach pronounced, and then, with newfound diplomacy, hastily added, "except for you guys, of course."

Josh's report: Aced his physics exam, Lexie's mother

had invited him for dinner tonight (and he had tentatively accepted, awaiting full parental approval), and Mrs. Harris across the street had her baby, and the boys had seen her and agreed that she was nothing special to look at. Plus, her name was Willow, and how random was that? Michael and I exchanged glances. We recognized the technique — bury the topic of keenest interest in the middle between good news (physics exam) and light gossip (new baby, named for a tree) in hopes of mindless parental nods of agreement.

"Pending a positive report from Anya," I said, "dinner with Lexie's family is fine."

Josh barely controlled a look of triumph and shot his brother a look that clearly communicated, "Told you I could do it!"

Within a few minutes we were awash in a counterpane of toast crumbs, and the boys had clattered back downstairs. I surveyed the mess on the bed. "Do you think there's any chance all those dandelion seeds will embed themselves in the toast crumbs, and we'll be sprouting weeds here in bed?"

"You're the gardener," said Michael. "But offhand, I'm not sure there's enough substance in the crumbs, unless you consider the dog hair part of the planting mix."

He swung his legs over the bed, the remote temporarily abandoned and the sound of all-sports-all-the-time not yet disturbing the morning.

"Shower dibs first," he said. "Hey, why'd you ask me about going to a wedding when you woke up?"

"I woke up with that beautiful wedding march in my head — not the usual, the other one."

"You know, Mags, as a mere mortal, I'm not sure I can guess what 'the other one' might be."

"Okay, it's not dum-dum-de-dum."

"Not 'Here Comes the Bride'?"

"Other one. Trumpet voluntary...."

"Am in the shower. Let me know when you figure it out. Or stop being such a know-it-all and Google it like a normal person."

"Normal is for chickens!" I shouted. No answer. I heard the water running and happily gathered all the pillows to enjoy on my own. I glanced over at my nightstand. iPhone 6 right there, every trumpet voluntary known to humankind and pluckable from memory with just a quick search. I lay back on the pillows — mine, all mine — and just let go, looking up at the ceiling to see what would come up. Google indeed. Google was for amateurs. *Cinderella*? Was there some *Cinderella* wedding march? Nope, getting it mixed up with the *Sleeping Beauty* waltz. Cinderella's prince? And then it popped up as if it were painted on the ceiling. I threw off the covers, stalked into the bathroom, and opened the shower door.

"Maggie, shut the door! You're letting in cold air."

" 'Prince of Denmark's Wedding March,' " I announced and closed the door. I picked up my phone, searched the piece, flopped back on the pillows, and let the music wash over me. "Baroque, originally attributed to Purcell, but actually composed by Jeremiah Clarke," I reported to no one in particular. "Ah, Maggie, you've still got it."

Michael came out of the bathroom, wrapped in a towel. "Are you out here congratulating yourself?"

"I am. You are so lucky."

"Really? Shove over, let's see just how lucky I am."

"Not that kind of lucky, I've got a million things to do — and so do you."

"Don't you miss morning sex?" he said wistfully.

"I do," I said, heading for the shower. "But the boys have soccer practice, and I want you to help me liberate that old steamer trunk from the laundry room, since Beau thought some of Alma's papers might be in there. And we already know that Alma and Victoria were close, so maybe that will tell us something."

Michael followed me into the bathroom, stood at the sink, and half-heartedly lathered up to shave.

"I thought the term was 'soccer mom.' How did your sexy Italian lover turn into a pedestrian soccer dad? You got my hopes up with that Princely Danish."

I laughed. "I think you've just reduced one of the great Baroque pieces of music into a pastry." I turned on the water and shed my nightgown. Michael caught my eye in the mirror.

"Not too late," he said. "Shower sex isn't half bad."

"Later, Lothario." I hummed the "Prince of Denmark's Wedding March" with a darn fine imitation of heavenly trumpets, just slightly off key.

CHAPTER 35

MAGGIE
OAKLAND

The soccer dad good-naturedly tugged Alma's trunk into a clear space in the laundry room.

"Hey," he said, "what a coincidence. We've got about five loads of laundry to do, so you can conduct your research and run a whole bunch of laundry at the same time."

"How convenient is that?"

With that, the boys were off, the washing machine was on load number one, and I perched on a folding camp chair to tackle the footlocker. It had lived in our family room for years, standing in for a coffee table we'd never gotten around to buying. It had been my grandmother's going-off-to-war trunk, made of metal, scratched but barely dented, with reinforcing bands of brass. I'd always been reluctant to open it, because eau de mothballs still escaped whenever the lid was propped open. I'd tossed in scented soaps over the years, trying to fight the moths with more pleasant fragrances, but most of the time, it had just been the thing for the boys to prop their feet on while they ate popcorn during family movie nights. Later, it got exiled to the laundry room.

I wrinkled my nose and lifted the lid, expecting more stale smells to creep into the laundry room. Instead, a faint scent of lavender wafted out.

"Lavender soap," I said out loud. "Thank you for vanquishing the mothballs." I removed the soaps and layer by layer began deconstructing Alma's memories. Right under the soaps was a layer of old tea towels, soft white linen with red stripes. When I lifted them off, the first thing I saw was familiar — Alma's dress uniform, olive drab, with her captain's bars still in place. I remembered trying on the jacket as a little girl and asking her to teach me how to march. She good-naturedly led me around her kitchen, through the living room, and out to the backyard. I followed her like a silly duckling, trying to keep up with her crisp commands. When I lost my place, we both dissolved in giggles, and then we saluted each other and marched right back to the kitchen table for lemonade and a big bowl of sweet Rainier cherries.

And here was her jacket. I held the inside of the jacket close to my face and just breathed. Beneath the old mothballs, beneath the lavender, I thought I caught a whiff of Shalimar, the perfume Alma had loved.

The washing machine spun itself to quiet. I hung Alma's jacket on a padded hanger so it would keep me company while I continued to unpack.

Here's what I discovered: envelopes of photographs, some of Alma and her fellow nurses in uniform, some of them on the wards, many on the hospital ships, some on trains. There was a glamour shot of Alma with a very young Morris, holding hands at a nightclub in New York. He was in uniform; she was in a full-skirted red dress, with a sweetheart neck, and a close-fitting black cocktail hat adorned with a handful of red feathers.

Some of these photos I'd seen in Papa Morris's albums, where he had lovingly created book after book of homages to his beautiful wife.

Here was my favorite discovery: a blurry, typed document entitled "Packing Suggestions for Nurses Sailing to Europe."

1. *Trunk locker (weight limit 85 lbs). Bedding roll, not over 50 lbs. One piece of hand luggage, not more than 40 lbs. One field or musette bag. Each individual must have a duffel bag to be placed inside bedding roll. Total not to exceed 175 lbs in weight. Your musette bag will serve as an overnight bag or emergency kit.*

2. *When packing, consider your needs for the voyage. These are to be packed in your handbag and musette bag. These two pieces are to be taken with you aboard ship. Note: You will be toting your own bag, so bear that in mind. Your foot lockers and bedding rolls will be stowed in the hold of the ship and will not be accessible.*

3. *On boarding, your ship uniform will include the olive drab winter uniform, gas mask, helmet, musette bag, and pistol belt with first aid pouch and canteen. The field coat and handbag are all that will be carried, unless you have a musical instrument that you wish to take. When traveling to port, dress in full uniform and remember that you do not appear as an individual but are representing the Army Nurse Corps, and the 191st General Hospital.*

The public not only observes you closely but critically.

4. *We will see you at the port. Remember security for both yourself and your unit. Do not say "Goodbye" as such a remark always invites questions.*

"Mom, Mom, where are you?" I heard Zach call. "We're starving!" I looked up from the list, still many pieces of advice to go.

"I'll be up in a minute," I shouted back, thereby breaking yet another impossible-to-keep Fiori house rule: Don't shout between floors. I heard Michael's low voice, issuing instructions about cleaning cleats outside and handwashing, and the sounds of the fridge opening and closing. There was life overhead in all its details, large and small, but I couldn't quite bear the thought of tearing myself away from Alma's footlocker.

Michael came to the top of the basement stairs. "Everything okay down there, *cara*? I don't hear any washer or dryer sounds?"

"Just between loads," I said, with a guilty look at the washer and dryer. I tossed the wet clothes into the dryer and dumped a load of sheets and towels into the washer.

I carefully smoothed Alma's list, brought it upstairs, and listened to the soccer highlights — Zach had a "clean sheet" as keeper, with no goals scored on his watch, and Josh got a goal and was thrilled that Lexie had (a) come to the game, (b) seen him score, and (c) invited him to her game.

Michael handed me the cutting board, celery, and a knife, and I heard the rest of Josh's recital — Lexie,

Lexie, Lexie, midfield move, Lexie, Lexie, Lexie, idiot striker, and, by the way, he and Lexie were going to be just like Alex Morgan and Servando Carrasco.

Michael and I exchanged glances. "The soccer stars," he explained, "who just got married."

"Another victory for same-sex marriage in sports," I observed, believing that every moment is a teachable moment.

Josh groaned. "Alex Morgan is a girl, and she was the star of the 2012 Summer Olympics. She's a striker and she made a goal in extra time that won the game. Aced out the Canadians."

"Oh well, another victory for women athletes."

Josh rolled his eyes. "Mom, you know, *everything* in the world isn't about a life lesson."

This was going well. "So, what about the guy — Carrasco?"

"He played for the Houston Dynamo," said Michael, adding, sotto voce, "that's an MLS team, not a nuclear reactor."

"But now he plays for Sporting Kansas City and he's a midfielder, like me," said Josh.

"Listen, buddy," said Michael. "I wish you and Lexie every good fortune in pursuing those big-time soccer careers. Your mother and I will be all primed to accept your offer of early retirement for us with gratitude and enthusiasm."

Over lunch — gallons of orange juice for the soccer stars, tuna sandwiches (cut on the diagonal for Josh and as rectangles for Zach, can't remember why), apples, and at least one giant bag of pita chips — I pulled out Alma's list and read it aloud to Michael and the boys.

"Wow," said Josh, "talk about a lot of rules and regulations."

"They were sailing away from home, and there wasn't going to be a Target or a supermarket on the ocean or once they'd landed."

Michael was leaning over my shoulder, reading ahead. "Hey, I love this stuff. Listen to this — 'Manicuring sets, yes, but polish brighter than Windsor is taboo in some theaters.' "

"Theaters?" asked Zach. "They were going to work in movie theaters?"

"That's what they called areas of operations — the European theater, the Pacific theater, and so on," I said. "It's a kind of taxonomy, a way to organize and subdivide military operations. So, you start with the war, then go to the theater, and then to a campaign. For example, in the European Theater, where Alma was sent, there was the Western Front and the Eastern Front."

Josh looked up. "Hey, we do that in biology — we classify organisms through taxonomy. Like kingdom, phylum, class, order, blah, blah, blah."

"Yeah," said Zach. "Like you're the ruler of the Dunce Kingdom."

I expected shoving and insult-trading to ensue. Instead, Josh patted Zach on the head. "Doesn't matter, I'm still the ruler of something, doofus, so just get in line or I'll exile you."

By now, Michael had claimed possession of Alma's list. "Here's some more cool stuff. 'Curtains: Colonel Martha Clements has suggested that each nurse take a few yards of some gay material with which to brighten up her quarters.' And how about this? 'Kotex: Take a

two-month supply, part of this to go in your hand luggage. Colonel Clements's suggestion is to have on hand
four to five made of diaper material, just in case.' "

"Double gross," said Josh. "And besides, nobody
uses that stuff anymore." I waited politely, suspecting
there was more coming. "Lexie uses...oh, never mind...."
Even in our oversharing household, this was a little too
much detail. Still, I would have relished overhearing
the conversation between Josh and Lexie when this information was transmitted. Zach looked mildly puzzled
and not particularly interested.

"Here's my favorite, slightly cryptic item on the
list," Michael pressed on. " 'Watch: Can you depend on
yours?' "

"I do love this list," I said, clearing dishes and dis-
patching the boys to homework. "Finish everything up
so it's not hanging over your heads on Sunday," I called
as they clattered upstairs. "And we can have pizza and a
movie night." In an instant, the kitchen was silent.

"I know what you mean," said Michael. "I feel as if
we're seeing a whole forgotten world unfold — and it
makes me realize how much guts it took to leave behind
everything familiar and set out on that journey."

True to form, Michael was busy architecturally reorganizing the dishwasher. "Hey," he said, "are you going back to Alma's trunk? I could help for a while, if you
like. Divide and conquer?"

"Delightful. Just remember that he who assists in
the history excavation will also find himself adjacent to
the dryer."

"Good. I'm a far superior folder."

CHAPTER 36

MAGGIE
OAKLAND

> *"I looked at my hands to see if I was the same person. There was such a glory over everything. The sun came up like gold through the trees, and I felt like I was in heaven."*
>
> — Harriet Tubman

I had to give Michael credit. His lawyerly skills of discovery turned out to be quite useful. He rescued a half dozen empty banker boxes from the garage and labeled each box: Alma, Alma and Morris, Victoria, or ??

"What are the question marks?" I asked.

"We don't know what it is yet, so you reserve extra boxes to create new categories as they become apparent. You touch each piece of paper *once* and decide what it is and where it goes."

"I had no idea being a lawyer was so boring."

"At work I have indentured servants, otherwise known as associates and interns, who do the most boring stuff. But it's good to know how to tackle discovery in an orderly way, no matter how brilliant and important you are."

He fished another camp chair out of the bowels of a crammed laundry room closet, and he divvied up what I'd already gone through.

"I've already looked through that whole stack," I protested.

"Right," said Michael. "But did you look at every page? And did you place everything in categories?"

I could see that accepting "assistance" had its downside.

"And to get us in the mood," he said, punching buttons on his phone, "a new Pandora station of Southern-flavored music."

With that, "Stars Fell on Alabama" began competing with the sounds of the washer and the dryer.

Two hours of meticulous reading and sorting, leavened by Elvis, Johnny Cash, Muddy Waters, Loretta Lynn, Patsy Cline, the Dixie Chicks, the Blind Boys of Alabama, Kings of Leon, and the Avett Brothers, yielded tidy boxes of Alma, Alma and Morris, Alma's recipes (which turned out to be one of the ?? categories), and only a few letters from Alma to Victoria, written onboard the hospital ship, the *Charles A. Stafford.*

"Your grandfather was a player in his day," said Michael, holding up one of Alma's letters. "Listen to this:

"Dear Morris, I hope that your excursion is going well, and I look forward to your return in a few weeks. I must thank you [I guess!] for arranging such lovely entertainment while you are away. Every single afternoon I receive an invitation under my door requesting that I dine below deck as Cookie's personal guest. Of course, I

am not foolish enough to turn down those invitations; he always has some delectable treats tucked away for his guests. I know that I had to "slide through" since I did not weigh quite the requisite one hundred pounds when I joined the Army Nurse Corps, but I do not think you need take responsibility to pile all that extra avoirdupois on me during one journey! Oh, yes, I know you are behind these invitations, and Cookie has made it clear that he has been deputized to make sure I receive his personal attention. Funny, between work and these lovely dinners, I have not had time to visit with any other officers. Surely that could not be your intention? With affection, Alma."

"Papa Morris told me that story," I said. "He was best buddies with the chef or the cook or whatever you call that guy who cooks on a ship, and I think he had a little black-market business on the side procuring really good steaks for his favorites — which included Papa Morris, because once in a while he let Cookie win a pool game. Anyway, Cookie had promised Morris to keep Alma very busy whenever Morris had to go ashore for a few days."

"And he kept his word," said Michael. "Okay, anything left in the trunk?" He peered inside, reached down to the bottom, and came up with a dark-brown velvet bag. "I've seen this before."

"It's the prayer shawl Papa Morris's father gave to him on his bar mitzvah," I said. "I'd lost track of it. Papa Morris wanted to make sure it went to one of the boys after he is gone."

Michael placed the bag on my lap. "Will he mind if the great-grandson who inherits the prayer shawl has not been bar mitzvahed?"

"I asked him that," I said, "when he was still pretty with it. He said that both the boys had good hearts and that was enough for him."

Willie Nelson and the spin of the washer finished at the same moment. Michael got up to make the transfer. I sat with the bag on my lap, thinking about how easy it is to lose things. "Elizabeth Bishop," I said. "She's the poet who wrote about losing things." I put both hands on the soft velvet, tracing the embroidered Hebrew letters I could no longer remember.

"Can I have your phone?" I asked Michael. "I need to look something up."

He handed it over. "Hallelujah, the girl is mortal," he announced to the laundry room.

"The art of losing isn't hard to master;
so many things seem filled with the intent
to be lost that their loss is no disaster.

Lose something every day. Accept the fluster
of lost door keys, the hour badly spent.
The art of losing isn't hard to master.

Then practice losing farther, losing faster:
faces, and names, and where it was you meant
to travel. None of these will bring disaster.

I lost my mother's watch. And look! my last, or
next-to-last, of three loved houses went.

The art of losing isn't hard to master.

I lost two cities, lovely ones. And, vaster,
some realms I owned, two rivers, a continent.
I miss them, but it wasn't a disaster.

— Even losing you (the joking voice, a gesture
I love) I shan't have lied. It's evident
the art of losing's not too hard to master
though it may look like (*Write* it!) like disaster."

My face was wet. "I am just an emotional shipwreck."

Michael closed the trunk and sat on top of it. He said, "No handkerchiefs in the laundry — but lots of cloth napkins."

He dabbed at my face with one of my mother's old linen napkins.

"You haven't lost the prayer shawl," he said. "Can I see it?"

I nodded and reached inside and pulled out the *tallit*. White wool spilled across my lap, and the *tzitzit* untangled.

"It's in perfect condition," said Michael.

"Put it on."

"I don't know. I think putting something this sacred around the shoulders of a fallen Catholic is not, well, kosher."

He picked up the brown velvet bag, which still had a certain heft to it, and handed it to me. "There must be something else in there. Why don't you check it out?"

Michael lifted the shawl from my lap, shook it out, and laid it on top of the dryer. I put my hand back in the bag and pulled out a small, flat wooden box. I opened it and fanned three photographs on top of the footlocker.

Michael pointed to each one. "It's you," he said. "And again. And again."

The first photograph was a hand-tinted formal portrait of Jules and Victoria, she in an elegant, hoop-skirted lavender gown, he in white tie and tails. Jules was almost precisely her height, and he looked not at the camera but at her, clearly wondering at his good fortune. Victoria looked straight ahead, gazing into the camera with the carriage of a queen. I turned the photograph over. *Victoria and Jules, February 14, 1867*

The second was an untinted photograph of Victoria and Eli, he looking like the cat that ate the canary, with a very large serving of cream on the side, and Victoria looking solemn, with her hand tucked decorously into his arm. They were standing on the Oxford courthouse steps, squinting a little in the sun. She was in a simple narrow dress, embroidered on the bodice, and the skirt falling straight to the floor. Eli, clearly a man with a taste for style, sported a brocade vest underneath his cutaway jacket.

On the reverse of the photo, *Victoria and Eli, March, 1863*

Michael picked up the third photograph and handed it to me. "This is what you've been looking for: Victoria's first love." In a forest, four solemn people stared straight ahead. The bride and groom sat on a fallen log, holding hands. The bride wore a dark dress that fell in soft folds; the groom, a well-fitted coat and cravat.

"That's the dress," I said, reaching out as if I could

feel the fabric. "The dress that Gabriel's sister, Sarah, made for Victoria. It must be — it looks like midnight blue, and it drapes like velvet. I read about it in one of Victoria's letters to Gabriel."

"Tall and princely," said Michael, nodding at Gabriel's likeness. "And I see there must have been music." At Gabriel's side was his horn. "Who are these other folks?"

"I looked at the man standing next to Victoria and knew in an instant. "It's her brother, Jeremiah. See, he's got a wooden leg."

"But he didn't approve of their relationship, right?"

"I guess he rose to the occasion. But it looks as if he came alone — no wife, no parents."

"Probably didn't want to involve or endanger anyone else."

I put my finger on the young woman standing next to Gabriel. "And my guess is that's Sarah, the dress-maker."

"So they had witnesses," said Michael. "They were not alone."

"It's what Stephen Sondheim says in *Into the Woods*, 'No one is alone.'"

Michael put his arm around me. "Uh-oh, that song makes you weepy. Dissolves you into a puddle."

"Does not!" I protested, as my eyes welled. "I just find it comforting."

"Where's the officiant?" asked Michael, reaching over to reclaim the linen napkin for me.

"I bet there wasn't one. I've read about this — you know that 'jumping the broom' thing? Turns out that a couple could be married either through a Scripture wedding, where they each read some passage of Scripture to each other, or by jumping the broom."

"Look at that," said Michael. "In the background."

I held the photo closer — against the trunk stood a simple broom. "And Gabriel's sister is holding a Bible."

On the back of the photo, in ink, I saw:

V and G, we are blessed

CHAPTER 37

VICTORIA TO GABRIEL, 1864

My love,

Every wonder in my life comes back to you. I had felt at-
traction to young men before you, I had even flirted with
those whom I found witty or clever or charming. But love,
now that is an entirely different matter. Today, you have
shown me another wonder: how wide and magnificent
the world can look when we are drifting overhead. I never
imagined that my disguise as Virgil would yield this unique
experience, standing by your side in the basket of a surveillance balloon. My heart beat so fast when you brought me
to the launch site, not because I was afraid of heights, but
because I didn't know if your story about training me as a
backup telegraph operator would be believable. But your
Mr. Pinkerton seemed eager and completely unperturbed,
complimenting you on your foresight. I didn't know where
to look when you were unspooling that fanciful story. And
then, Mr. Pinkerton had more questions. Where had we
met? How did I learn my trade at such a young age? How
did I feel about going up in the air? I answered his questions,
focused on breathing in and out, slowly and regularly, the

same technique I employed when riding with the Cavalry. The more frightening the encounters, the more I concentrated on slowing my breath. At the end, though, I think I strayed too close to the truth. "Gabriel is a skilled teacher," I said. "I am not afraid when I am in his hands." Your face was impassive. You and I both knew what risks we were taking, but on we went.

At first I was startled by the sound of the hydrogen generators roaring as they slowly, slowly inflated the balloons. Then, with your assistance, I scrambled into the basket of the *Intrepid*, and with two aeronauts aboard, off we went. I was at your side, ostensibly observing the telegraphic process up in the air, but truly marveling at what we saw from 500, then 1,000 feet above the ground. I had heard so much from you about Professor Lowe and his genius, but now I was experiencing it! And you were right, I was not frightened or giddy, not a bit. I was thrilled. I cannot wait until this war is over and we can share more adventures.

All my love, V

CHAPTER 38

MAGGIE
SAN FRANCISCO

Reentry is always an adventure. The stack of folders on my desk was approaching Leaning Tower status. Gertie, my assistant, critic, and official "Mum" of the *Small Town* wolfpack, had printed out a one-page summary of emails she considered urgent, cheerily color-coded, escalating from blue to yellow to red. "You know," I protested, "I actually look at my emails when I'm away."

"Just a convenience," she said. "That way I don't lose track of anything either."

I handed over a box of pralines. "Thanks for minding the store."

She took the box with a grimace. "Thanks for sabotaging my diet." She looked over her shoulder. "Hoyt's hovering."

"Hoyt," I shouted. "Come in quick or Gertie will start lecturing me about any number of things I've left undone."

Hoyt came to the door, armed with two cups of coffee, eyed Gertie's box of pralines, and stood by my visitor chair. "Oh, go ahead and sit," said Gertie. "I'm the kind of Midwest broad you shouldn't waste all that chivalry on."

I reached out my hand and Hoyt delivered the coffee, precisely the color of caramel I liked, enough cream so that I believed I was ingesting some essential Vitamin D. "Bless you," I said.

Calvin stuck his head in the door and, without an invitation, came in and collapsed on the tiny couch against the wall, his legs draped over the arm rest on one end. "Make yourself at home," I said tartly.

I delivered Hotty Toddy tea towels to Hoyt. He lit up. "These are perfect!" And I handed Calvin a box of Phoebe's cheese straws.

"Fat pills," he said. "Also perfect. Now, let's hear all the family gossip. You know, you should think about taking me with you next time — stir up some gossip about you philandering again, this time with some preppy darkie."

Hoyt shook his head. "Calvin, do you *ever* think before speaking?"

"Advantage of being an independent contractor," he said. "Although I willingly slave for *Small Town* in whatever photographic trenches you toss me into, I am, happily, not on the payroll."

I glanced at my watch. "I've got twenty minutes before my first fabulous date this morning with our accountant."

"Tell all," said Hoyt. "We want the gossip, the food report, celebrity sightings, and most of all, what you found out about the mysterious Victoria."

"Plastic surgery has made inroads into Oxford, Mississippi, with women in dark glasses spotted skulking around the Square. The whole pop-up tent thing in the Grove is weird but convenient. Aunt Phoebe treated us like we'd just been liberated from a prison camp for an-orexics. We had meat and many, many sides. Every day, every meal. Saw two Manning guys at City Grocery, and Morgan Freeman at Ravine. Oh, and Ole Miss lost the Egg Bowl...."

"...but won the party," said Hoyt. "Come on, tell us about your mystery ancestor."

"In a nutshell —" I stopped. How to tell Victoria's story — or at least what I know of it — in anything re-motely resembling a nutshell?

"Let me put it this way. I think Victoria must have been the gutsiest person ever. She defied her family to become a nurse, and she worked at the Confederate hospitals — the biggest one, Chimborazo. And then she switched sides. She got married three times — twice for love, I believe, and once for protection. She went to jail for being a spy."

"Oh, my," said Hoyt. "This is a story."

"There's more," I said. "She also disguised herself as a man and joined the Cavalry, with her horse, Cour-age. Oh, and then there's Gabriel, the great love of her life and husband number two. He was black, which was considered immoral and illegal six ways to Sunday."

"She married a brother?" asked Calvin. "In the 1860s? Sounds like she was the one who should have been named Courage."

"Or Gabriel should have," I said. "He would have been the one likeliest to get strung up on a convenient tree."

"Love," said Calvin. "It's a dangerous thing. But you've got to hand it to the both of them — willing to take such crazy risks." He shook his head. "But what about the time she didn't marry for love? What was that all about?"

"Childhood friend, who grew up to be something of a wheeler-dealer. He lent money to the Confederacy to finance their blockade-running, but if I understand things correctly, he did that just to get some inside info. He was a Union sympathizer, even though he'd grown up in Oxford, Mississippi — which is how his family and Victoria's family knew each other. And he's the one who recruited Victoria as a spy and introduced her to Rose Greenhow, the notorious flirt and Rebel loyalist."

"Greenhow," said Hoyt, "I know who she was. There's a book about her — one of my aunts bought it for me at the International Spy Museum in DC. Went to prison with her youngest daughter, right?"

"Yep," I said. "Little Rose was nearly as much of an operator as her mother. But things didn't end well for Mrs. Greenhow. After she was released from prison, she was exiled to the Confederacy, which suited her just fine. She had stashed Little Rose in the Convent of the Sacred Heart in Paris — and then the fearless Mrs. Greenhow made the mistake of stepping onto the *Condor*, a blockade-runner headed to Bermuda, Halifax, and Wilmington, North Carolina."

I took a sip of coffee. "I can finish telling you about this later. I know we've got a crazy day."

"Are you nuts?" said Calvin. "Finish the story."

"So...first the *Condor* ran into bad weather, and then it ran into a Union gunboat. Rose practically ordered the captain to lower a lifeboat. He resisted, but Rose could be persuasive, and so she and two other Confederate agents set out in a small lifeboat on bad seas." I sighed. "They only had two hundred yards to go, but the boat overturned, and Rose and her accomplices had to swim for shore. She was a good swimmer, but she was wearing a heavy dress and carrying a bag of gold coins tied around her waist, supposedly money she'd been paid for the memoir she'd written, *My Imprisonment*."

Hoyt said, "She drowned."

I nodded. "She did. Her compatriots made it to shore, and Rose's grand plans to deliver critical information to Jefferson Davis were dashed." I took a sip of my coffee. Heaven is a stimulant. "But you have to give her credit — she never gave up her cause."

"I'm still thinking about the poor schlub Victoria married that she didn't love. Probably carrying a torch for her all those years, and then she just used him." Calvin sat up. "By the way, Maggie, you need a new sofa — this one is way too short for proper lounging."

"Feel free to run right over to Macy's and purchase a new one. Using your credit card. And by the way, I think the 'using' was mutual. Married women were not nearly as suspect as single ones — in some ways, they had far more freedom than their unmarried counterparts. And they had the 'protection' of a husband. I think Eli Mays — that was Victoria's first husband, the childhood pal — greatly benefited from Victoria's spying activities. He traded in information, and she provided it."

"Speaking of protection," said Calvin. "Assuming Victoria and Eli consummated their unromantic union, what did people in the Civil War era do about not making babies?"

"I think that's a story all by itself," I said. "Turns out that some version of condoms and of diaphragms were already in use in the nineteenth century."

"Made of *what*?" asked Calvin.

"Well, rubber was involved. I think it was the modern evolution of the famous French letter. Instead of sheepskin and other yukky animal membranes, Charles Goodyear vulcanized rubber, which made it more durable and flexible. Though from what I've read, these nineteenth-century condoms were not one-time, use-and-discard deals. You had to clean them out and use them again and again."

"Yeech," said Calvin. "I like you empowered feminists with your handy-dandy birth control pills."

"Of course you do," I retorted. "And you'll be happy to know, there were all kinds of rubber-product versions for the ladies. My favorite was something called the 'womb veil.' I was telling Michael about this, and he said it sounded to him like a really untrustworthy temporary patch you'd put on an inner tube."

"I'm hoping we're moving on to a different subject soon," said Hoyt.

"I've gotten way too interested in this whole Civil War–era contraception subject," I said. "I've got an idea for a *Small Town* story."

The room grew quiet. "You think I'm nuts, don't you? But here's my idea: We call it *Devices and Desires* — you know, that P.D. James novel that featured her poet-policeman, Adam Dalgliesh. I think human beings have always been looking for the next great answer to how they can have consequence-free sex. I mean, Margaret Sanger didn't invent the term 'birth control' until about the time of World War I, but for thousands of years — literally — people have been trying to figure it out."

"Sounds like a history piece to me," said Hoyt. "Not quite what our readers are interested in."

"I beg to differ. We're all about what's going on in our 'small town,' what's new, what's trending, etcetera, etcetera. In fact, right now, there's a little movement to return to more 'natural' methods of birth control. I mean, I can't believe it, but apparently there are some hipsters who are out there advocating for the strategically timed pull-out. And the rhythm method."

I scanned Hoyt's and Calvin's faces. Calvin was horrified. Hoyt looked puzzled.

Gertie stuck her head in. "Five minutes to come-to-Jesus time with the accountant." She glanced around the room. "What are you guys discussing?"

"The rhythm method."

"Oh," she said, "my favorite method of birth control."

"Really? Why?" I asked.

"It gave me both my sons. Doesn't *prevent* anything, just appears to facilitate the whole process for a Catholic girl like me."

"And on that note, back to work," I said.

Calvin fell into step with me as I headed down the hall. "Hey, Mags," he said. "Were you kidding about the devices and desires story? If you're not, I've got some great ideas about doing some way-out-there photos."

"Not really," I said. "I haven't thought it through yet, but there's something in the idea that we can have all these lofty thoughts and feelings — passion, love, betrayal, sorrow — and at the end of the day, there's this practical element. Victoria was conflicted about the war, but she made a choice, and that choice involved masquerading as a Cavalry soldier. So she did it! She dressed as a young man, she rode into battle, she gathered information, and it must have been useful."

"I'm not following what that has to do with being practical?"

I grabbed Calvin's arm. "It's everything. It's Victoria learning spycraft from Mrs. Greenhow. It's Eli sending her out riding without a bonnet or gloves to roughen her skin. It's figuring out how to not get pregnant — until she wanted to. After all, she slept with three men: Eli as a comrade, Gabriel as her true love, and Jules as her husband and the man who made her a mother and a grandmother and a great-grandmother. It's Rose Greenhow dying because she *didn't* think through the practicalities of swimming to shore in a heavy dress with a sack of gold tied around her waist."

"What about the marriage between Gabriel and Victoria?" asked Calvin. "That was nuts, and I say that as a brother who believes in love. There was nothing practical in it — they took terrible risks. Don't you think that if Gabriel hadn't gone down in the balloon, he'd have been strung up for defiling a white woman?"

"Ah," I said, "that's why this is such a good story. For all their passion, they were careful people — not because they were afraid, I think, but because they wanted to protect each other. We don't really know where they had their assignations, but my guess is that Gabriel's sister, Sarah, provided them shelter. She was a seamstress and a young widow, and she lived alone in the woods. No one would have noticed if her brother and a friend were visiting."

"How much of that are you making up, Maggie?"

I shrugged. "Some of it. Not all. I know she was a

seamstress. She made the dress Victoria got married in."

We arrived at the conference room. I gave a little wave to Mr. Lofter, our accountant. I know he had a first name, but all of us called him Mr. Lofter. Or sir, if we were worried.

"Don't you think it's peculiar that your accountant's last name is *laughter*?" asked Calvin. "Have you ever heard him actually laugh?"

"Nope. Consistency is his middle name. And his last name, by the way, is *not* laughter, it's pronounced 'lofter.'"

"Whatev," said Calvin. "Hey, you said you had some pix I could look at — where are they? I'll see if the grand master of the lens —"

"That would be you, I'm assuming?"

"None other. I'll see if I can get some more info from the photos."

"Calvin, wait a minute," I said. "There's something I didn't talk about."

"Okay — spill the beans."

"Victoria killed a man."

"Whoa. Who? Why?"

"Don't know his name. He stumbled upon Victoria and Gabriel together in the woods. She managed to get the guy's rifle and threatened to shoot him."

"She made good on that threat?"

"Yes," I said. "And saved Gabriel's life and probably her own."

Calvin shook his head and put his arm around me. "You come from tough stock. Out in the woods it must have been do or die."

"Victoria went with 'do,'" I said.

CHAPTER 39

MAGGIE
SAN FRANCISCO

Mr. Lofter had news far less dire than I had imagined. He approved of my byzantine machinations to get nonprofit media foundations to underwrite special research projects and fund interns. He didn't approve of our business itself, of course, and certainly not of the frothy nature of our magazine. He also complimented me — and the publisher, who, sadly, had disappeared to get an adult beverage and was unlikely to return in the next twenty-four hours — on holding costs down. "Silly extravagance to have people on staff," he said. "Benefits and all that. I like your model."

"We do have staff," I protested.

"Yes, but you have independent contractors as well, especially those photographers and stylists and illustrators. Keeps the overhead low."

"Well, thank you, I guess."

"I do wonder, Mrs. Fiori," he said, "why you all soldier on in a dying industry. Really, there must be easier, more lucrative ways to make a living."

Things were going well. It did not seem like the moment to engage in a defense of *Small Town*, to confess that I loved our silly little magazine. I loved all of the writers and the designers and the columnists and many of our readers. I loved the fact that within the pages of our magazine we covered not just fashion trends, gossip, and restaurants, but substance as well. We poked fun at the Twitterization of our beloved *Small Town*, aka San Francisco. We covered unlikely heroes like Grace Plummer, the murdered socialite who got her hands dirty teaching young women how to garden and how to feed themselves and their children. We were not *The Nation* or *Charlie Hebdo*, but we labored in our own field, watching out for the city we all loved. Of course this lovefest did not extend in every direction. I did not love Mr. Lofter, but I didn't think that was going to break his heart, and in my own bumbling way, I seemed to be keeping us more or less on budget.

"Now, if I were you, Mrs. Fiori, I'd be thinking about some very dramatic opportunities to cut costs."

"Oh, really?" I said, now feeling very ready to bid Mr. Lofter adieu. I glanced at my watch as non-discreetly as I could. "What did you have in mind?"

"You put your whole magazine out there on the internet. Maybe we don't even need a printed version. I'm always throwing out every magazine that comes in the house. It's just clutter. And the ink smells."

"Oh yes, Mr. Lofter, it does smell. It smells wonderful! And that's part of why we print the magazine. I was just wondering," I inquired innocently, "if you enjoyed receiving your complimentary subscription to *Small Town*? I started sending it as a gift to your wife, because she told me she enjoyed it so much but had to buy it on the newsstand."

"She was spending money on that thing?"

"Yes, many people do. That's why we still have advertisers and we're still in business."

He flushed. "Well, thank you for your time, today, Mrs. Fiori. And congratulations. You're the first editor I've worked with who could read a balance sheet."

He left. I put my head down on the table, not sure whether to go seek somebody to high-five with or simply have a brief, delicious, quiet nap.

CHAPTER 40

MAGGIE
OAKLAND

By the time I stopped at the grocery store and picked Zach up from goalkeeper practice, it was already 6:30. I tossed the mail on the dining room table and called upstairs. "Helloooo up there?"

"Josh? Michael?" Silence. And then I heard laughter on the front porch. I opened the front door to see Josh and Lexie locking their bikes. Immediately I was on RoboMomCop alert. Where had they been? What were they doing?

"Hello, Mrs. Fiori," said Lexie, taking off her bike helmet and shaking out what Josh referred to as her "hot hair." "Hey, I like your flower."

I was puzzled for a moment until she gestured toward my shoulder and I realized she was talking about the felt flower Zach had given me for Mother's Day. She leaned closer, "Wow," she said. "Pistils and stamens and everything. Very cool."

"Lexie's like you, Mom," said Josh. "She knows a whole bunch of goofy stuff." I started to say that anyone who'd taken any science classes *at all* would know what a pistil and stamen were, but in some miracle of restraint I stopped myself.

And suddenly I felt the rare sense of knots loosening inside me. Lexie and Josh were just a teenage version of all of us who fell in love — sweet, naïve, lost in each other. Maybe it would last. Probably not. But my great-great-great-grandmother Victoria would not have approved of squelching young love.

"Come on in," I said. "You guys must be hungry. And Lexie, please call me Maggie. When I hear Mrs. Fiori, I think someone's talking about my mother-in-law."

"We're not really hungry," said Josh. "We did our volunteer shift at the Food Bank, and they always bribe us with cookies."

"Well, I'm starving," confessed Lexie. "I didn't like any of those cookies."

And so the lovebirds settled around the kitchen table and ate half a loaf of Michael's banana bread and polished off all but one of the tangerines, which disappeared as soon as Zach came tumbling downstairs.

"Lexie," I said, "why don't you check in with your folks and see if it's okay to join us for dinner?" Of course she texted rather than called, and her mom responded in the affirmative in less than a minute. Grudgingly, I was beginning to see the finer points of texting compared to actual voice-to-voice human contact. Human beings, human voices: Who needed all that extra embroidery on relationships?

Dinner...hmmm. I opened the fridge, resolving once again to reform instantly, overnight, into one of those plan-ahead moms. Surely there was some large pot of cassoulet in there, just awaiting a warm-up. Had Michael and I discussed a dinner plan and I missed it?

My cell beeped in my pocket. Message from Michael: *I want something spicy for dinner. Picking up Thai. Home in 15. Is Lexie-the-cupcake joining us?* Message from me: *Lexie is joining us. We need to be more respectful of her. Time to retire the cupcake title.* Message from Michael: *Who are you? And what have you done with my snarky wife?*

With dinner on its way, I turned to the day's pile of mail: junk, junk, junk, catalog, catalog, catalog, and a package! From Beau.

Zach came into the dining room and leaned on my shoulder. "Can I hang out with you, Mom?" he asked. "Josh and Lexie are doing homework in his room."

"Absolutely. You're practically my favorite hang-out date, but don't tell your father or Josh. They've got a very low jealousy threshold. Hey, remember when Aunt Phoebe sent me those cool photos that set Dad and me off on our big quest to Oxford?"

He nodded, "That was *sweet*. I love having a mystery in our own family. And now you and Dad have sorta solved it, right?"

"Well, we know a lot more about Victoria — that's what Dad and I were talking about at dinner with you guys last night. That she was a nurse and a hero, she disguised herself so she could go into battle like a man, and learned information that helped the Union soldiers win the war — and put an end to slavery. And she secretly married a black man who worked for the Union. But there are still things we don't know. We know she was in some very important battles, but we don't know all of them. She was friends with a very famous poet, Walt Whitman, but we don't know if they stayed friends until he died. He was much older than Victoria, so he died about fifty years before she did."

I picked up the package Beau had sent and began slipping the twine off the wrapping. "But you know what? This whole adventure began with a package from Aunt Phoebe and Uncle Beau."

We unfolded the paper and the bubble wrap layer, and once again, there was a soft, brown leather book inside, along with an envelope from Beau. "Is this going to be another poetry book?" groaned Zach, clearly disappointed that there wasn't spygear of some kind in the package.

"Let's see what Beau has to say." I picked up Beau's letter and read it aloud:

"Dear Maggie, Phoebe and I enjoyed seeing you and Michael in our little town. Although Phoebe still feels apologetic that she didn't cook something Italian to honor Michael's heritage. She says to tell Michael that she is working on her gnocchi and will have a treat for him next time. I cannot tell you how much it means to me that you are interested in our family's history — and how impressed I am with the way you figure things out. When you deduced that Virgil Alexander Cranston was a nom de guerre for Victoria Alma Cardworthy, I knew that you deserved to know everything I know about Victoria."

Zach pointed at "nom de guerre," dashed off boldly in Beau's quick strokes. "What does that mean, Mom?"

"Literally it means a 'war name,' but it's often used to mean just another name someone might assume because they're playing a role they don't usually play."

"But Victoria did have a real name and a fake name for when she went to war, right? That was her soldier name."

"That's right, honey. So, in this instance Victoria really did have a nom de guerre, in the middle of a war." I read him more from Beau's letter:

"This little book is a record of every battle where Victoria was involved. And, it took me a while, but over the years, I've managed to decode Victoria's notations, with some help from the Mississippi Historical Society. I don't think you'll need any help in deciphering it, and I think that will be much more enjoyable to you than if I sent you the cipher key for her messages. If you get stuck, call me. I will give you two hints now. One, it's a standard alphabet manipulation cipher, and two, the music is in the name and the name is in the music.

"Phoebe and I send our love, and we hope that you will return to see us and cheer on Ole Miss again."

I opened the book and saw that it was a kind of miniature ledger, a row of primitive pictographs across the top: a horse, a soldier's cap, a crutch, a tombstone. Below each image there was a number. And below that was some incomprehensible code.

"Whoa," said Zach. "Mom, how are you going to figure that out?"

"Beats me, buddy, but I'll give it a try." The door opened and Michael struggled in, holding two enormous brown paper bags, a bakery box, and his briefcase.

"Thai me up, Thai me down," he said. "Dinner has arrived."

Within minutes the table was set and the myriad white boxes emptied into bowls, sending fragrant whiffs of deliciousness into the air. No need to call anyone for dinner — Josh and Lexie followed their noses and migrated downstairs immediately, Zach was already seated at his place, chopsticks in hand.

Josh cleared his throat and stood up. "I think we should have a toast. To Mom and Dad coming home and to Lexie for making this a perfect dinner." Michael and I did not make eye contact. Of course, Josh was showing off for Lexie, but still — a classy thing to do. We all raised our glasses — sparkling cider for the kids, a lovely but affordable Oregon pinot noir for us. Josh, ever the lawyer's son, did try to make the case that he and Lexie should be drinking whatever we had in our glasses, but no dice. I know sophisticated French or Italian parents would mix wine and water together for their kids, and think that was no big deal, but I didn't want to deliver Lexie back to her parents in anything resembling an altered state.

Over dinner, I explained the cipher-breaking challenge Beau had set before us. "I don't get it," said Josh. "Beau knows the cipher info, so why doesn't he just send it you?"

"Where's the sport in that?" asked Michael. "Beau's thrown down the gauntlet. He's provided some clues, and he thinks we can figure it out. Well, he thinks Mom can figure it out, but we know she needs her crack team of consultants." He gestured around the table with his chopsticks.

"Not tonight," said Josh. "Lexie and I have tons of homework."

"Saturday morning then," I said. "Waffles and bacon at nine to sustain us. I'll do some research on how the standard codes and ciphers work, and then we can dive in."

CHAPTER 41

MAGGIE
OAKLAND

"I'm trying to channel Alan Turing," said Michael. "Brilliant, eccentric, thinking outside the box."

"Persecuted, misunderstood, not so great with human interactions," I countered. "But keep channeling the brilliant part."

Lexie had shown up at the door, cheerful, hungry, and ready to go. I relished seeing a beautiful young woman who seemed to have no food issues. She'd brought her laptop, and on it, she'd installed software that allowed you to launch any alphabet manipulation — advance ten letters, for example, so that A became J, B became K, and so on.

After breakfast, we moved to the family room — or, as Michael kept referring to it, the "war room."

We decided to start with the cipher and tackle the code-breaking later. "Point of information," said Michael. "Maggie, you were going to explain the difference between code and cipher before we dive into this."

"And I am ready to deliver. Khan Academy was my go-to spot, because I think their folks are great 'explainers.' Basically, codes are a kind of shorthand, taking a longer, more complicated word and creating a meaningful shorter phrase. It's both a way to hide information and a way to shorten the time and space a message takes up — hence, Morse code. But you need a codebook to deconstruct the meaning, or it has to be intuitive in some way. Ciphering is much simpler — essentially you just pick a number, and you can shift a letter forward or backward by that number. The example Khan Academy uses is how, by shifting each letter by three, you can turn Hello into Khoor and vice versa."

On a big Post-it easel sheet, we wrote all the names that seemed like possibilities to launch our de-ciphering quest.

Victoria Cardworthy, Eli Mays, Gabriel Hunter, Sarah Hunter, Jeremiah Cardworthy, Walt Whitman.

"How did you figure out Gabriel's last name?" asked Michael. "I never saw it mentioned in any of letters between Gabriel and Victoria."

"I made the same journey that Alma and Victoria did just before Alma went off to war — I went to the cemetery in Oxford early one morning with Beau. I'm sure that Hunter was the last name of Gabriel's master — that was often how slaves were named. But Gabriel kept it after he bought his freedom and became a telegraph operator, so either he liked the name well enough or he had grown accustomed to it. So that's the name that's on his gravestone."

"So, Mom," said Josh, "how do we factor in the music angle? Uncle Beau said, 'The name is in the music, the music is in the name.' What does that mean?"

"No idea, unless there's a way to find something musical encoded in somebody's name. We know that Victoria liked to sing, as did Gabriel, and maybe Gabriel's

sister, Sarah, sang as well. Plus, there was Walt Whitman and his 'Song of Myself' — references to singing
are in many of his poems. Oh, and Eli! In one of Victoria's journal entries she writes about the songs she and
Eli used to make up."

"But Gabriel is the only one who really was a musician, as far as we know, right?" asked Michael. "He
had a horn — a bugle or a trumpet or some other brass
instrument."

"Duh," I said. "Of course. You're right! So, since it's
an alphabet cipher, maybe we should do some variations
on his name and try shifting a number that's part of his
name. In other words, Gabriel would mean that we'd
shift the alphabet seven letters, Gabriel Hunter would
mean we'd shift it thirteen letters. But just so we don't
miss anything, maybe one of us should do Walt and one
should do Walt Whitman — Victoria clearly admired
him, and there's all that 'I sing the body electric' stuff."

Josh had created electronic alphabet squares for all
of us so we could try different names without wasting
paper. "Sustainable detective work," said Lexie. The girl
was growing on me.

Michael, Josh, Lexie, and I worked on our laptops;
Zach used his iPad. Michael took Gabriel, I took Gabriel
Hunter, Lexie took Walt, Josh took Walt Whitman, and,
just to cover the bases, Zach took horn.

Counting the letters was a little tedious, but once
we got the hang of it, it went quickly. But by mid-morn-
ing, it was clear we didn't have a winner.

"We could call Beau and ask for another hint," suggested Michael.

"No!" said everyone else, including me. "Can't give

up this easily."

Lexie said, "Okay, what if 'name' means the name of a person and the name of a song or an instrument?"

"Good thought — like Nellie Bly Victoria or Song of Myself Whitman or Gabriel's Horn?" I said. We all started scribbling variations, counting letters, and testing the ciphers. Lunchtime came and went. Finally, at 1:30, as the allegedly responsible mom in the room, I called time out, and we broke for haute cuisine: tuna sandwiches.

In the middle of lunch, Zach asked to be excused. "You haven't finished," I said. "Code and cipher breakers have to keep their strength up."

"I'll be right back. I need to do something." He picked up his iPad, now even grimier than usual, the screen covered with a faint film of mayonnaise, and went back into the family room.

The rest of us brainstormed other combos: Victoria and Nellie, Transcendental Walt...we were down to ideas that were lame and lamer.

Suddenly, Zach reappeared in the doorway, pumping his fist in victory. He turned his iPad around, and before our eyes, the ciphers were understandable:

Chancellorsville, We began on April 30, we ended on May 6. Merciful God was nowhere in sight. Every day more gruesome than the one before. Thanks to the brilliance of General Lee and mistakes by General Hooker, the Confederacy prevailed. But early in this terrible battle, the Union had a bright spot at Jenkins Ferry. The Second Kansas Colored Volunteers attacked with fierceness and courage, seeking

revenge for the many colored casualties in the
Union engagement at Poison Springs. Union
casualties: 1,694 killed, 9,672 wounded, 5,938
missing and captured. Confederate casualties:
1,724 killed, 9,233 wounded, 2,503 missing and
captured.

Zach put the iPad down on the table and took a deep bow as we all applauded him. "Mrs. Fiori," said Michael, "I believe there's a new know-it-all in the house." We all bombarded Zach with questions. He held up his hand, enjoying the theatrical moment.

"The idea of the instrument and the name was right. We just didn't have the right combination. I tried Gabriel's horn, but I didn't know what to use for the apostrophe. So I tried Horn of Gabriel, thirteen letters, and it worked. How did you know it would be thirteen letters, Mom?"

"I didn't! I just used that as an example because there are thirteen letters in Gabriel Hunter."

"You da man, baby brother," said Josh. "Maybe you'll make something of yourself some day."

Zach turned a deep, delighted shade of red. Praise from Josh was equivalent to winning the Nobel Prize.

"Mom," said Josh, "where's that little book? I have an idea about what those pictures and numbers stand for." I put a Xerox copy of the first page on the table — no need to take chances with mayonnaise migrating onto a 150-plus-year-old notebook.

"Look — the crutch must mean casualties. The numbers are the same as in the deciphered info. The tombstones mean deaths, the soldier's cap may mean how many people are still standing after a battle." He thought for a moment. "I don't get what the horse means."

"Maybe the number of cavalry troops?" said Lexie. "When we studied the Civil War, I remember reading how important horses were and how many were killed in battles."

"Plus," I said, "Victoria — as Virgil — joined a Cavalry regiment, so she would have been particularly concerned about keeping track of horses."

We spent the rest of the afternoon decoding the images and deciphering the little book. But thrilling as it was to be able to read Victoria's notations, battle by battle, the grimness of what we were reading made the room grow quieter and quieter. One after another, the battles took lives: the Battle of Franklin, the terrible losses of Pickett's Charge of the West, the cavalry-against-cavalry of Trevilians...page after page of casualties, deaths, and then, one day, a personally heartbreaking entry from Victoria: *Who am I without my Courage? He fell today, shot through his great heart. But even in his last moments, Courage looked out for me. He fell so slowly, so gently that I was unhurt in body, although I was deeply hurt in spirit. Farewell, good friend.*

Josh read this passage aloud, his voice breaking at the end. He stood up abruptly and left the room. Zach burst into tears, and Lexie put her arm around him.

"Josh," called Michael. "Come back a minute. We want to be together and think about Victoria and Courage for a few minutes." Josh came back, clearly worried that some cheesy sentimental something was going to happen.

I glanced at Michael. He gave me his trademark 'I've got this under control' look. I hoped he was right.

"There are so many reasons war is terrible," he said. "And we hope you never know that firsthand. Mom and I were spared that, but you know that Alma and Morris served in World War II, and Victoria and Courage served heroically in the Civil War. You guys honor them when you learn about history — and when we learn from history."

"Okay, Dad," said Josh. "We get it. And it seems weird to get so wigged out about a horse dying — a long, long time ago, when there were thousands and thousands of people dying."

"You remember what that vet at UC Davis told us when Raider was sick and we were all so upset?" I asked. "She said, 'Love is love. There is no hierarchy.' I think we all reacted so strongly to Courage dying because Victoria loved him, and they were together through thick and thin." I took a deep breath. "I think it's time to call Uncle Beau and let him know that your generation — Zach, Lexie, Josh — solved the puzzle. And then, it's time to figure out where we want to go to dinner to celebrate tonight."

The kids called Beau, since it was their victory, while Michael and I convened in the bedroom. "Holy crap," he said. "That went to a pretty dark place. Think we're terrible parents? Think we need to call Lexie's folks?"

"Chill pill," I said. "I see little historians in the making. I wish someone had brought history to life like that for me when I was their age."

"Hope you're right," said Michael.

"Let's go somewhere Eye-talian. We'll make up for

Beau and Phoebe overlooking your culinary heritage. And let's invite Lexie's folks so we can demonstrate how normal we are."

"Uh-huh. I guess it's my job to lead the charge on the 'we're normal' front. And I call Pizzaiolo on the Eye-talian front."

CHAPTER 42

VICTORIA'S JOURNAL, 1864

Tomorrow, they will come for me. I am not afraid of prison, but I am afraid that I will not see the man I love again in this lifetime. This is what frightens me, that I have endangered the living creatures who mean the most to me. Eli has been most heroic, considering that I know his so-called friends are making cruel sport of him. He brought me dinner last night, since those self-important fools have confined me to home arrest until I am remanded to jail. Afterward, he told me he stopped at Old Greeley's tavern for refreshment. This morning, he brought me flowers and reported on his misadventures at Greeley's. He said the entire crowded, noisy room grew silent as a church when he walked in. I want to write down what he told me, every bitter word, so that if I ever leave prison, I will think more deeply about what consequences my behavior can have on others.

"Vic, you would have laughed. That buffoon Charlie Carter stood up and put his pistol on the table, and he said, "We won't drink with a man who can't keep his woman away from the negro."

I buried my head in my hands. "I am so sorry, Eli. I never

meant to bring such misery on you."

Eli snorted. "Misery? You think I care what that fool declares?"

"What did you say?"

"I said, 'I wasn't planning to drink with any of the likes of you anyway. I prefer the company of my true friends. And with that, I pulled out a chair and sat down, and I said, 'Just in case there are true friends in this room, I have chairs enough for three of you at this table. If you join me, I am buying. We will be toasting the woman I love. All I can say is that any portion of my wife's affections is worth more than all the charms of a dozen lesser women.' "

I raised an eyebrow. "You did not really say that?"

"I did, indeed. I wanted to squash that blowhard Charlie Carter like the despicable bug that he is. Threatening me with a weapon!"

"Well," I said, "he wasn't exactly threatening you, if he laid his gun on the table."

Eli laughed. "How quickly you get over your repentance, dear Vic."

"Don't leave me in suspense," I countered. "Did anyone come over to your table?"

"Why, yes. John Graves, sitting right next to Charlie. He stood up, told Charlie not to be such a horse's ass, walked over to my table, and sat down and said, 'I'm not dumb enough to keep company with Charlie Cartwright, and I'm sure as hell not dumb enough to turn down a free drink.' "

"Anyone else?"

"John's three-legged dog followed him over to the table. You know that flea-bitten old hunting dog he keeps? The one who got his leg caught in that coyote trap?"

I laughed. "That is one fine posse you gathered for yourself, Mr. Mays."

"I am glad, Mrs. Mays, that you approve of the company I keep."

CHAPTER 43

VICTORIA'S JOURNAL, 1865

When I came back from the prison hospital this afternoon, Eli was waiting for me with a grand bouquet of purple and white lilacs tied with satin ribbon.

"I have news, Mrs. Mays," he said. "The war is over, and you have been pardoned." I could not hear what he said; it made no sense to me. I began to sway, and just before I fainted, Eli dropped the bouquet and caught me in his arms.

When I came to, I was on the rough cot in my small bedroom. Eli was sitting on a low stool next to me. I had "graduated" to trusty-dom, as had all the nurses in the prison hospital, so I no longer lived behind bars. But for more than a year, I had known nothing but the prison hospital, the vegetable garden I helped cultivate, and occasional visits from Eli, my brother, Jeremiah, his wife, Elizabeth, and Gabriel's sister, Sarah.

Sarah and I had become friends. At first we were tied mostly by our sorrow, united in our grief over Gabriel's death. But as we grew to know and like each other in deeper ways, her friendship meant more and more to me.

Eli leaned over the bed. "Are you thirsty?" I nodded.

He brought me a cup of cool water and helped me sit up.

"Where are the lilacs?" I asked.

"Right next to you." I turned and saw them in a large jug on the floor, and I was wrapped in their beauty and fragrance.

I held out my hand. He took it in his and brought it to his lips.

"Thank you, Eli," I said. "Can I really leave? Stand up and walk out of here?"

"You can. After all, you are no longer a bigamist, since Gabriel is...gone. You have been pardoned as thanks for your service to the injured and to the Union.

"And not that you care a whit about this," he added, "but the charges of miscegenation against you have been removed."

I sat up and tidied my hair. "You are right. I do not care a whit about those ridiculous and immoral charges. Telling people who they can and cannot love."

Eli laughed. "I believe that what you mean, Mrs. Mays, is that you do not care a whit about what anyone says you can or cannot do about *anything*."

I smiled. "You are so correct, Mr. Mays."

And with that, my first husband escorted me to one of the finest hotels in Washington, DC. I had a bath, we had dinner, and I began to think about the next chapter of my life. I would divorce Eli, of course. Ours had been a marriage of convenience, although to my surprise, I had found some passion and great affection in our relationship.

Eli would protest, but I would ask him for a divorce. He deserved to be married to someone who loved him above all others.

I found it hard to believe that I would find love ever again. Gabriel was everything to me. But I am an optimist. I know that love is essential to human beings, and I wanted to believe that it would come my way again.

Our terrible war ended on April 9. It was spring, and there were lilacs, and I was free. Jeremiah and Elizabeth were expecting their first child. There was, despite so much loss and grief, some spring sense that there might be, as the Bible says, "joy in the morning." Lilacs are a good start. With time, we will be our United States again, I hope and believe. I want to be ready when that joy comes around again.

CHAPTER 43

MAGGIE
OAKLAND

I was mulching the front beds, smeared with dirt and more than a little sweaty, when Calvin and Andrea pulled up to the curb.

Andrea was in half-prep: Levis, cuff-linked linen shirt, and a cashmere sweater; Calvin in full prep, from the Burberry cap on his head to the penny loafers on his feet. More to the point, they were both clean — everything I was not.

They surveyed me with suspicion. "It's called gardening," I said. "A person gets dirty." Calvin and Andrea were shacking up in a pristine condo many stories above where dirt lives.

"I'd give you a hug," said Calvin, "but yuck. No thanks."

"Come on in. I'm ready to take a shower, and you guys can have coffee and some very nice brownies Michael made."

"We brought you a present," said Andrea, "but you can't have it until you're clean. Really."

Michael roused himself from football to put on the coffee and entertain our visitors while I hosed off.

"Okay," I said. "Pony up the present. I'm practically

pristine."

"Remember those three photos you showed me a few weeks ago?" asked Calvin. "The ones of Victoria and her three husbands? There was something very interesting about the way the photo in the woods was posed, the one with Gabriel and Victoria. It was...well, nowadays, we'd say it was art directed. So I went to a couple of online photo archives and turned up a whole bunch of Civil War–era photos. Mathew Brady was the famous dude who photographed the Civil War. You've probably seen lots of his photos in the Ken Burns documentary. But there were other photographers as well, and one of them had this very distinctive style, and something in it reminded me of Gabriel and Victoria's wedding picture."

"Enough talk," said Andrea. "Show them the book."

Calvin pulled a hardbound book out of his portfolio case and put it on the table. "Apple books," said Calvin. "Instant miracles. I use the same approach, I'm just more...you know...."

"Full of yourself," said Andrea.

"Talented is what I was going to say."

"You're killing me," I said. "Open the book!"

Victoria and Gabriel's wedding shot opened the book — Calvin had clearly done some restoration and enhancement, and the photograph glowed.

"It's beautiful," I said.

"Wait, there's more." He turned the next page, and there was a balloon basket with three people on board, and the balloon was just starting to rise into the sky. I recognized two of the three people — Victoria (in disguise) and Gabriel.

"I can't believe this photograph even exists," I said.

"We don't know the name of this photographer — all the attributions for his shots say 'unknown artist' — but apparently he was very interested in science and new-fangled things. And there are so many photos of Gabriel that I think the two of them must have been friends or worked together or something." Calvin turned the page, and there was Gabriel at the telegraph office, up in the balloon again, operating the telegraph, and helping to tie down the balloon at the end of a flight. On the last page, Gabriel held his horn.

"Victoria would love this," I said. "I know that's a crazy thing to say, but it's not just that she would have loved seeing these photos after Gabriel was killed. It's that she could share Gabriel with the rest of us."

Michael said, "Man, this is the coolest gift ever. I am going to opt out of the whole gift-giving sweepstakes for the rest of my life."

"Okay," I said. "Maybe you are a genius, Calvin."

"I'm thinking," he said, "that it's possible these photos might have a little more appeal than your whack-job Civil War–era primitive contraceptive shots, with a little sheepskin on the side."

"How do we package the story?" asked Andrea. "Besides the fact that they're photos of people Maggie wished she'd known in person...."

"Unknown artist capturing nineteenth-century innovation and technology," Calvin retorted.

"And you like that better than my womb veil?"

He did. We talked Hoyt into a photo essay, and when it came out in *Small Town*, one of the chichi photography galleries in Hayes Valley decided to mount a show of the images. Mr. Lofter was thrilled when we invited him to the opening. I'm not sure how wild he was about the photographs, but he enjoyed the free wine and tapas. "The gallery's paying for the refreshments, right?" he asked. We'll turn him into a culture vulture yet.

Meanwhile, Calvin's on a roll. Now he's scouring more databases to find images of Victoria. I'm glad he's looking, but I already have the one I love. It's the daguerreotype Beau and Phoebe sent me all those months ago, of Victoria on Courage, ready for whatever came her way — in love and war and love, again.

EPILOGUE

MAGGIE, SIX MONTHS LATER

Calvin and Andrea invited us to dinner last night. They're both good cooks, they live in a soothingly child- and dog-free place, and they spend money on good wine. Who could say no?

As we sat down, Calvin remained standing. He put his hands on Andrea's shoulders. He cleared his throat. "We have some news."

"You're getting married," I blurted. "It's about time."

Now Andrea cleared her throat, audibly. "We already did," she said. "About a year ago."

"Congratulations," said Michael. "That's wonderful! He turned to me and said pointedly, "It's just terrific, isn't it, Maggie?"

My eyes welled with tears. "I wanted to dance at your wedding," I blubbered. "I wanted to throw you one of those awful showers and play stupid games." I gathered myself, stood, swiping at my nose, and hugged them both.

Andrea started to laugh. "I'm sorry, I knew you'd be mad. We just wanted to get married quietly without having all that awful big-white-wedding folderol. So we decided to be just like Eli and Victoria and marched ourselves over to City Hall and got married by a justice of the peace."

"Okay," I said. "I may forgive you, but I get to throw you a party."

Calvin said, "For the record, I love a big white wedding." He held up his hand. "Ignore that opening."

"You can certainly throw a party for us," said Andrea. "And meanwhile, you're going to have to traipse to Connecticut, because my mother is throwing a party as well." She paused. "But maybe you want to plan a different kind of party."

"Anything you want," I said. "I don't really like those stupid shower games anyway."

Michael snorted. "You do, too. You're so competitive that even when you're the hostess you have to win everything."

Calvin brought in a bottle of champagne and poured all of us full glasses, and then put a splash in Andrea's flute.

I looked at Andrea and I looked at the glass. "I'm throwing a baby shower, aren't I?"

Calvin and Andrea both got the giggles, and everyone started talking all at once. "I knew you'd figure it out," she said.

Baby Storch-Bright was born twenty-four hours after what was, I must admit, a spectacular baby shower. He weighed in at a robust eight pounds, beautiful in every aspect. His mom and dad named him Gabriel.

ACKNOWLEDGMENTS

This story is entirely fictitious, but it was inspired by two real-life heroes: my mother, Vauneta Cardwell Winthrop, and her older sister, Virginia Cardwell Mc-Duff. They were both captains in the Army Nurse Corps during and immediately after World War II, and they both served in the European theater. They grew up on a family farm in Mississippi during the Depression, and when they were both young (ages ten and twelve), their mother died. My mom and Aunt Ginny helped raise the four younger siblings and then put their younger sister through college. They didn't have the same kind of adventures that Victoria did, but they had plenty of their own.

They were both beauties, inside and out. Aunt Ginny had a compelling low-pitched Tallulah Bankhead voice and was a great success in community theater. On a family trip, she showed up in a backless green-silk evening gown, and let's just say my stylish younger sister and I were no match for Aunt Ginny's razzle-dazzle. My mother, Vauneta, equally beautiful, captivated her patients. One of our family treasures is a dramatic pencil sketch of our mom sitting on an unnamed beach. She had taken a group of recovering patients there, and one, especially smitten, had turned his ardor into art. Another had carved a jewelry box for her and lined it with soft red cloth, and today, that box sits on my dresser. My father worshipped her, and even in her late seventies — after forty-plus years of a storybook marriage — he would sigh and fret that someone might take her away from him. In a sense, my parents' marriage inspired this book. I've always been interested in unlikely couples. My mother was a Southern Baptist farmer's daughter from Lambert, Mississippi. My father, five years her junior, was the son of a Romanian Orthodox Jew and was raised in Providence, Rhode Island. Love is crazy, isn't it? And sometimes the crazy works out.

They are all gone now — my father, who introduced me to Dashiell Hammett's mysteries, my beautiful mother, Aunt Ginny, and her husband, Mac, along with all the other Cardwell siblings.

I do have to give a shout-out to my late Uncle Ed, the youngest Cardwell sib and, like his fictional counterpoint, Beau, the family genealogist. Uncle Ed was an example of the complexity of the South. He attended the University of Mississippi; a few years later, as a member of the National Guard, he was back on campus to protect James Meredith and the other African-American students gutsy enough to start integrating Ole Miss.

And for those of you fortunate enough to have enjoyed Southern cuisine, you should know that Uncle Ed's widow, our Aunt Florice, is a consummate hostess with an abundant pantry, great skills, and a generous heart. I was channeling Florice when I created Phoebe.

Thanks have to go out to the Spy Museum in Washington, DC. Its exhibition on women spies, particularly in the Civil War, set me on this journey. Of course, women spies have shown up in virtually every American era since the Revolutionary War. However, the Civil War generated a remarkable collection of women who were spies for the Union and the Confederacy. The audacity of these women is remarkable, given that they plied their trade in times when it took very little to bring ruin to a woman's name.

Many thanks to my cousins, particularly Janie Cardwell, Diane McDuff Johnson, and Anne Cole Billings, all of whom helped me navigate Oxford's history, charms, traditions, and food. My cousin Diane is a wonderful discovery partner, whether roaming around Faulkner's Rowan Oaks or filling me in on the latest news about the cousins. Anne's lovely daughter, Mimi, is now at Ole Miss, so the circle continues unbroken.

My support posse remains steadfast. Excellent readers and writers cheered me on: Ann Appert, Kathy Bowles, Betsy Brown and Lulu Brown, Caity Burrows, Fred D'Orazio and Evan Young, Margret Elson, Scott Hafner and Bill Glenn, Kathy Halland, Maria Hjelm, Wendy Lichtman, Karen Mulvaney, Phyllis Peacock, Ben and Kate Peterson, Michele Siegfried, and the late Steve Tollefson, who even in the hereafter still hopes I'll write — or at least read — an epic Norwegian saga. My high school bestie, Emily Stevens, is always thinking of new readers who *must* meet Maggie. And I confess to my other high school pal, Richard Wells, that when I write I am trying hard not to disappoint him. And though his career has been in television, those of us who admire him know that he is the real deal in writing. I have been blessed by knowing one of the world's most elegant curators of good reading, Delwin Rimbey. Special thanks to Nancy Buck and Laurene Mullen, who not only read but also made suggestions so useful that I expect them to send me an invoice any day now. Gratitude to Sydney Kapchan, who connected me with Larry Bruiser, who introduced me to Louisa May Alcott's first-person accounts of nursing in the Union Hospital at Georgetown. And kudos to my Stanford pals, who are legion and loyal: the Grillos, the Hothans, the Heywoods, Paula Fitzgerald and Chris Nielsen, Judy Heller, Lisa Lapin, Edie Barry, Carol Sisk, Duncan Beardsley, and many more.

Fellow mystery writers have been generous: Bob Dugoni, Jonnie Jacobs, Jon Jefferson, Susan Shea, Sheldon Siegel, Jackie Winspear, and Naomi Hirahara in particular. Plus, Naomi introduced me to two people whose DNA influences every cool mystery gathering known to humankind: Toby and Bill Gottfried.

It's a lucky girl who benefits from the loyalty of two book clubs. The first is my San Francisco Bay Area group: Johanna Clark, Janis Medina, Pam Miller, and Ellen Zucker; the second is my beloved Portland gang: Susan Aldrich, Peggy Almon, Karen Halloran, Joni Hartmann, Susan Hartnett, Laurene Mullen, Nanwei Su, Sandra Tetzloff, and Joyce Wilson. Always and forever, I'm indebted to my friend and designer extraordinaire, Jacqueline Jones (www.jacquelinejonesdesign), who generously supports Maggie's misadventures in every way, including the www.lindaleepeterson.com website. And I'm grateful to my business partner, David Skolnick, who made me get serious about mystery writing by sending me to the Book Passage mystery writers' conference years ago.

This book would not have happened without the encouragement, enthusiasm, and, when needed, bullying of Tom Clarke. When I was maundering on about how on earth I could pick up the pace and actually complete the book in about a year, Tom came up with a brutal — but very effective — solution. "Two chapters every two weeks," he said. "Send them to me." He had structured a wickedly successful set of threats so that I did, in fact, meet almost all my deadlines. Tom and his (much kinder) wife, Pat, kept me on track. I can't thank you both enough!

Lucky stars aligned many years ago when Amy Rennert agreed to be my agent. Her savvy, enthusiasm, and advocacy are something to behold, plus there's the extra bonus of volunteer counsel from Louise Kollenbaum, who knows what does or doesn't make a cover work.

My friends at Prospect Park Books are champions: responsive, creative, helpful at every stage, and just plain fun to be with. Thank you Colleen Dunn Bates and Patty O'Sullivan for everything. And a great big thanks to Caitlin Ek, who knows her way around bookstores.

Here's the criteria for being in our family: You've got to like books, theater, music, and movies; you've got to be able to cook (or at least be an appreciative eater); and you've got to run a mutual support operation. I am eternally grateful to my Peterson, Borden, and Sable in-laws for reading — and forgiving — Maggie. I am grateful to the small but mighty Winthrop clan, comprising my brother, Larry, sister-in-law, Pat, and my sister, Laurie. They are all fine readers and writers and even finer wielders of pom-poms — from Phoenix to Geneva, they cheer for Maggie and me. Thanks aren't enough.

My husband, Ken, says he often pictures our house, all three stories of it, being filled with words created by the three resident writers, circling up the stairs, dancing, searching for a fellow adjective or adverb. I guess they must float up, up into the air and escape out into the Portland sky, whether it's bright blue or leaden gray. I am so happy to be surrounded by great readers (Ken and our daughter-in-law, Kate) and writers (Ken, Kate, and, most of all, our son, Ben). Grandson Will, age nine, is so comfortable with our *lingua franca* that, at age seven, he cheerfully dispossessed his father of the microphone at a wedding to deliver an elegant and charming toast to the bride.

Of course, all this bibliophilia was launched by my parents. One of our favorite photographs of them was taken on the US Army hospital ship *Charles A. Stafford* at the end of the war. Both had some off-duty time, and a friend photographed them lounging on a blanket, nestled close to each other on what appeared to be a very hard, unforgiving deck. Both were grinning and just looking up from — what else? — their books.

Finally, writing about the Civil War is not for the faint of heart. The world is full of Civil War experts, amateur and professional, and only a fool would attempt to write about the era without being a serious scholar. In that equation, I am the fool, not the serious scholar. But I have tried to remain faithful to what we know of the times, the battles, and the unexpected heroes and heroines.

The sources that follow were invaluable to this rank amateur:

The Walt Whitman Quarterly, various issues

Stealing Secrets: How a Few Daring Women Deceived Generals, Impacted Battles, and Altered the Course of the Civil War, H. Donald Winkler, Cumberland House, 2010

Kate: The Journal of a Confederate Nurse, Kate Cumming, edited by Richard Barksdale Harwell, Louisiana State University Press, 1959

Walt Whitman's America, David S. Reynolds, Alfred A. Knopf, 1995

Walt Whitman: A Life, Justin Kaplan, Simon and Schuster, Inc., 1980

Hospital Sketches, Louisa May Alcott, James Redpath, 1863.

The Library of Congress Illustrated Timeline of the Civil War, Margaret E. Wagner, Little Brown and Co., 2011

Every Day by the Sun: A Memoir of the Faulkners of Mississippi, Dean Faulkner Wells, Crown, 2011

The Killer Angels, Michael Shaara, Crown, 1993

"What to Bring to a War: A Packing List for WWII Army Nurses List," provided by Patricia Britton, courtesy of her mother, Laura Rodriguez, who served from 1944–46 in the European theater, published by the Vault, Slate's history blog

ABOUT THE AUTHOR

Linda Lee Peterson is the author of two previous Maggie Fiori mysteries, *Edited to Death* and *The Devil's Interval,* as well as several nonfiction books, including *The Stanford Century, On Flowers* (Chronicle), and *Linens and Candles* (Harper Collins). She is also one of the founding partners of Peterson Skolnick & Dodge, a marketing communications firm that serves business, arts and culture, environmental, higher education, and health care clients around the United States. A long-time San Franciscan and an alumna of Stanford University, Peterson now lives in Portland, Oregon. Learn more at www.lindaleepeterson.com.